Death Without Passion

"Get out of my house!" she screamed. "And don't ever come back or I'll tell . . ."

She saw his eyes then and stopped short, her voice cut off by terror for her life that came too late. She turned and ran screaming for help, with him after her. She got as far as the kitchen. He caught her as she was running past the open cellar door. He caught her around the waist, swung her high in the air, and threw her with brutal force headfirst down the cellar stairs. She hit the cement floor with sickening force and lay crumpled and still, with blood pouring out of her head.

For a timeless interval he looked down at her. He had committed murder. But he felt nothing.

DORIS MILES DISNEY IS
THE QUEEN OF SUSPENSE

DORIS MILES DISNEY
NO NEXT OF KIN

ZEBRA BOOKS
KENSINGTON PUBLISHING CORP.

ZEBRA BOOKS

are published by

Kensington Publishing Corp.
475 Park Avenue South
New York, NY 10016

First Zebra Books printing: April, 1990

Printed in the United States of America

FOR THE HARDYS,
MARY AND CHUCK,
BIFF,
TOMMY AND STEVE,
WHO ARE VERY DEAR TO ME

September, 1954

The little boy looked back just once as they drove away. The Horbals, standing in the front yard, waved to him and he waved back. Then he faced forward, his sturdy little body erect, his legs straight out in front of him, not long enough to hang down over the edge of the car seat.

The girl at the wheel, Miss Lambert—to the Horbals—glanced at him. His face told her nothing of what his feelings were on leaving the farm that had been his home for nearly the whole five years of his life. But his coppery-brown eyes were wide and serious as if he sensed, at least a little, what a different world he was moving into today.

"Well," the girl said, giving him a smile.

His answering smile was tentative and a little shy. He held tight to his favorite toy, a grimy,

7

battered polka-dot dog she had brought him months ago.

They were on a narrow gravel road. Goldenrod and reddening sumac along the edges were reminders that the month was September. There were no other houses, only woodland and fields, for half a mile after they left the farm, whose isolation had been one of its major advantages from the girl's point of view. Then they passed another farm, deserted, its windows shuttered, grass grown tall in the yard. The little boy looked at it and spoke for the first time. "That used to be Bobby's house," he said.

"Bobby's? Oh yes."

Bobby had been the only playmate the little boy had ever had. Several months ago Bobby's father had given up the struggle to farm worn-out land and moved to California to try his luck at the aircraft factories.

"It was too bad Bobby moved away," the girl said. "I know you've missed him a lot."

The little boy, whose name was Greg, said nothing.

The girl sent him sidewise glances. Was his remark about Bobby a cry of regret for all that he was leaving behind him? There was no way to tell. He was a self-contained little boy, slow to express his deeper feelings. He'd lived too much in a solitary child's world. She must change all that. But gradually, not rushing him, not overwhelming him with new things in a new way of life. She had been building toward today for five years. Now that it was here she must make haste slowly, not try to buy his confidence with talk of doing this or that, the nice room he'd have, the new toys, the private kindergarten where he'd make new friends.

He had always seemed fond of her. Mrs. Horbal had often remarked on how much he looked forward to her visits. And this morning he had come with her without showing the least sign of reluctance or distrust.

But how much did that mean? Who knew what went on inside a child? Not even a mother who took care of her child from morning until night could know all of it. And she, a visitor in Greg's world up until now, what could she really be sure of?

She sighed, but only briefly, as hope replaced the moment of doubt. After all, they would be together from now on and she would expect nothing at the start except the right to take care of him, meet his every need to the best of her ability, and hope that in time she would earn his complete love and trust. That was the way it should be, the most she had the right to expect.

It was a lot. It was a dream come true. . . .

The gravel road ran into a blacktop that wound uphill and down through farm country to the town of Oldfield, a small place with a general store, gas station, Grange hall, town hall, houses, a few other buildings, a white-steepled church. It was soon behind the girl and the little boy, and presently they turned onto a main highway that led toward home, eighty miles away.

The thought of getting home raised familiar misgivings. What if her plans didn't work out? What if her father, after a few days, didn't fall in with the suggestion she would make to him?

She mustn't even think of such a thing, entertain for one moment the possibility of failure.

If it came, she would have to tell her father the truth.

She said, "There's a box of cookies in back, Greg. Do you suppose you can reach them if you kneel on the seat?"

"I guess so." He turned around but had to stand up to reach all the way over to the back seat. She steadied him with one hand and, when he sat down again, let him open the box himself. They were chocolate cookies, his favorite kind. He was polite. He offered them to her first.

A companionable quality came into their silence as they ate. "They're good, aren't they?" she said and didn't add "darling" as she wanted to do. She had called him "darling" and other affectionate names often enough; but not today when she mustn't rush him even in the smallest way.

She was bending over backward, being plain silly, she thought. But she felt so tight inside. Suppose she called him "darling" and couldn't stop, kept saying "darling, darling, my darling, my heart's darling," and all the pain of all the

10

years burst out of her in such tears as she had never let herself shed?

He gave her his shy smile again. "I like chocolate cookies better than any other kind."

"So do I. Let's have another."

He ate his with relish. She had to force hers down, dry and tasteless in her dry mouth.

It was worth the effort. The companionable quality in their silence deepened. He ate a third cooky. Then she said, "It's eleven o'clock. Perhaps it would be better if you didn't eat the rest until after lunch." She relented as his face fell. "Well, just one more."

He took one more and then dutifully closed the box and put it down on the seat between them.

The road was little traveled. By twelve o'clock they were across the Connecticut River and by twelve-thirty only twenty miles from home, on a shore road that sometimes ran close to the blue, whitecapped waters of the Sound and at other times gave them only distant glimpses of it.

It was ideal September weather, with a cloudless sky overhead showing depth on depth of light and air, just crisp enough to make her suit jacket and the little boy's pullover no burden.

They entered Broome's Cove, population eighteen thousand, according to a Chamber of Commerce sign on the highway. It was an old and wealthy town, once renowned as a port and nowadays a select summer resort with a small

11

industry or two to augment its prosperity.

The girl said, "Time for lunch," as they approached the business district. "Oh look!" she added, pointing to a banner strung above the road, depicting in vivid colors a clown with a megaphone announcing that the Broome's Cove Annual Fair was now in progress.

She read the announcement to the little boy, whose eyes grew big over the picture of the clown. "Will he be at the fair?"

"I should think so . . ." She hesitated, then thought, Why not? They could have lunch at the fair, look around, buy a few small things that would amuse him. They hadn't, after all, brought many of his toys from the Horbals' since he couldn't appear too lavishly provided for in the role she had assigned to him.

"Would you like to go?" she asked.

"Oh yes." His eyes shone.

So easily, so lightly the decision was made. They didn't even have to ask directions to the fair grounds. Posters served as guides through the town to a great old wooden summer hotel dating back to the eighties and turreted, gabled, and verandaed in the style of its era. It had been well kept up and with its private beach and acres of grounds it had a certain period charm, the girl thought, looking at it as they got out of the car in the parking area. During the summer months it was probably the mecca of substantial people who had been coming there for years.

12

Now closed for the season, the hotel had been opened again for the three-day annual fair sponsored by the town's service clubs to raise funds for the Broome's Cove Crippled Children's Home.

It was midday of the second day. The fair was in full swing as the girl, holding the little boy's hand, moved toward the hotel, making slow progress through the dense crowd, her comments lost in a babel of raucous cries from sideshow barkers, tinny music from the merry-go-round, shrieks and laughter from riders on the Ferris wheel, scooters, rotojets, and other amusement devices.

The little boy hung back as they went past this section of the grounds. Afterward, remembering it, she would torment herself with the thought that if they had only stopped then to take rides on everything, if they had only stopped—

But she led him on, conscientiously keeping in mind what Mrs. Horbal had said about how small a breakfast he had eaten on this eventful morning of his life and that, since then, he'd had nothing more than a few cookies during a ride of seventy miles. So she said, "I'm hungry, Greg, and you must be too. Let's have lunch first and see what's inside and then we'll come back here for rides."

He wasn't an aggressive little boy; or perhaps it was because he wasn't quite sure of his place in her life, his relationship with her; whatever his reason, he didn't argue or make any sort of protest. He looked back, but that was all.

They went on toward the hotel, coming to a halt when a small dog popped up in front of them, nuzzling against Greg who bent down in delight to pet it. "Look," he said, "he's got brown and white spots just like Tony."

"Yes," she agreed, recalling the Horbals' dog, dead of old age last spring.

Greg gave the dog a last hug and it scampered away. "He's a nice dog," he said, faintly wistful.

"Yes, he is."

She would get him a dog of his own as soon as his status was settled. He could take it to bed with him and everywhere he went.

She wanted to tell him this but kept it to herself. No promises yet, nothing that would seem to bribe him to be happy with her. Make haste slowly.

They went up the broad veranda steps and into the hotel.

It was jammed. Lunch was being served in the lounge and coffee shop by women's groups from Broome's Cove churches, the big main dining room, that also did duty in the summer season as a ballroom, being given over to the exhibits.

They had to stand in line for a table. As people pressed around them, Greg became almost lost to view in a forest of adult legs. "Are you all right?" She bent over him. "I don't see how you can get any air."

"I'm all right," he assured her and tightened his grip on his toy dog.

At last they were seated and served chicken shortcake, salad, apple pie with ice cream. When they left the dining room, she looked at her watch. It was almost one-thirty. By three or so they should be on their way. She meant to be home not long after four, and she'd have to drop off the car at the rental agency—she never drove her own to the Horbals'—take a cab to the parking lot where she'd left her car, and go home from there.

They went through the lobby to the dining room-ballroom, a huge room that took up the whole length of the building. Booths and exhibits lined the walls; the doorways and high ceiling were festooned with bunting; and above eye level the banners and insignia of the sponsoring groups formed a colorful frieze all the way around the room. Here, too, there was a crush of people, a noisy milling throng in which the girl and the little boy were immediately caught up.

Right away he was enchanted by two clowns turning somersaults on a dais at the far end of the room.

"Well, let's go look at them," she said.

They started toward them. But then a dairy exhibit, an automatic cow with a moving head, a swishing tail, and a window in its side that revealed milk endlessly churning caught his attention and he couldn't be budged until he had looked his fill and exchanged a fleeting smile with a little girl standing beside him.

They stopped next at a candy booth where he made it a weighty business to decide what he wanted and finally settled on a box of homemade fudge.

He found it awkward to handle along with his polka-dot dog. The girl offered to carry it for him. "Can we open it later?" he asked.

"Yes, of course. On the way home."

Home, she thought. From now on, his home, too, something he'd never really had.

Suddenly pandemonium broke out near them as someone let loose a cluster of balloons, and children, squealing with laughter, rushed about trying to capture them. The little boy made no move to join in the fun. He remained close to the girl, content to watch, enjoying it, though not only the balloon chase but everything within his ken from the point they had reached midway in the room. He drank it all in, the sights and sounds, the people, the doomed people in holiday mood, buying and selling, greeting friends, exclaiming over what a success the fair was, the best one ever, the biggest turnout they could remember for the Broome's Cove Annual Fair.

Presently the girl and the little boy went on past fancy work and cheese booths and a lumber company exhibit. A burst of applause came from the crowd around the dais as one of the clowns rode a tiny bicycle up and down a narrow ramp.

16

"Can't we hurry?" the little boy said.

"All right." She laughed. "Let's spread our wings and fly over everyone's head. That's the only way we can get there faster."

"Maybe Sammy could be one of my wings." He put the toy dog up on his shoulder.

"But you can't fly with one wing," she reminded him.

They were both laughing. In laughter they found a release for the tension that had been building up in them since early morning, and as it went on, having nothing to do with the mild joke they shared, they were enveloped suddenly in a sense of closeness, an identity of spirit, unconscious but instinctive on the little boy's part, both conscious and instinctive on the girl's. Her hand tightened over his. They looked at each other happily.

Up ahead, on the opposite side of the room, was a booth where homemade pastries were being sold. Like the others, it was decorated with green crepe paper and had a cheesecloth backdrop lettered with the name of the group sponsoring it. Cardboard cartons and sheets of wax paper were stacked on a bench behind the booth. The stack had just been replenished by a helper, a young man who paused to light a cigarette. He thought he shook out the match before he dropped it and walked away.

At first it seemed the match would burn itself out on the bare wood floor. But a crumpled sheet

17

of wax paper beside it caught fire and flared up into the cheesecloth backdrop.

The woman tending the booth had no customers at the moment. Her attention was centered on the antics of the clowns, while the flame devoured the cheesecloth and raced with lightning speed across the paper-trimmed frame of the booth to the sequined backdrop of the one next to it. In passing, a separate tongue of flame reached out to lick casually at the hem of the woman's dress and ran up it to the heavy bun of hair on her neck.

She flung up her hands and screamed, "I'm on fire! Help, help! I'm on fire!"

One of the double French doors in the room stood open on the veranda; the other was closed and never to be opened that day. Facing it was the entrance to the lobby, creating a crosscurrent of air, the ally of the fire.

Almost before people could whirl around toward the screaming woman, flames had swooped on to a third booth, up the wall to the frieze of banners and insignia, across the ceiling on a bridge of bunting, and, in a matter of seconds, running wild through the whole room rich in flammable prey.

The woman beat at her hair with her hands, and her screams rose to a pitch of madness as she became conscious of her blazing dress and tried to run. But there was nowhere to run to. A torch of fire, she was hemmed in by a swirling mass of people who, after the first moment of paralyzed horror, stampeded for the exits.

Only those nearest the two exits immediately available got out without incident. Then the mob spirit took over in a mindless struggle to escape.

At the double doors to the veranda people were flung against the closed half, wedged there, knocked down, and trampled upon by the frenzied pressure of those in back of them who, in turn, became part of the piled-up barricade.

At the lobby entrance the same scene was repeated. Although both the doors were open, the drapery around them saying "Welcome To The Broome's Cove Fair" went up in a blaze, and when people tried to draw back from it, they were knocked down and trampled upon.

The windows were blocked off by booths already aflame.

A few escaped through the kitchen door in the rear, near the dais where the clowns were performing. The clowns, in fact, scooped up three or four children close at hand and carried them to safety through it.

The fire roared and crackled, finding fresh fuel in the old, tinder-dry wood of the paneled walls. Pieces of blazing debris fell from the ceiling onto the pushing, screaming mob jammed beneath it.

A few people kept their heads and tried to stem the panic with shouts of "Steady! Steady! Take it easy, take your time!" But the mob was deaf as well as mindless; the brave, the level-headed were swallowed up in it and had no chance to make themselves heard.

The girl and the little boy were just beyond the midway point of the room when the stampede began. She dropped the box of candy and her pocketbook and caught him up in her arms.

"Hold tight to me," she said. "Hold tight . . ."

She stood stock still for a moment, trying to keep cool and weigh their chances. The mob was already sweeping toward the two exits at the front of the room. That way, it seemed to her, there was no chance at all. But she had noticed the rear door near the dais. If they kept out of the mainstream of flight, stayed close to the booths, they might be able to make their way to it.

She had never before been caught in a mob, though. She was underestimating its blind force as she began to edge forward, clutching the little boy to her, but with only one of his arms around her neck, the other still holding his toy dog. Afterward, she was to ask herself over and over if she might have saved him if only he had let go of the dog and clung to her with both arms around her neck.

There was no answer to the fruitless question. Many children that day were swept out of protecting arms and trampled and smothered underfoot.

Groping and choking her way through the billows of smoke that poured over them, she made a little progress at first. But as the frenzy mounted she had no chance at all; as well try to stand up against a rushing wall of surf as against the mob. It engulfed her, spun her around, and tore the little boy out of her arms.

Then she was screaming too, fighting and clawing, trying to reach him, lost to sight, lost forever. . . .

The mob bore her away toward the French doors and hurled her, senseless, on top of the pile of dead and dying barricading the closed half of it.

When she opened her eyes she was outdoors, lying on the ground. First she became aware of a tremendous amount of noise and confusion nearby and then of legs running back and forth past her through a pall of smoke. She hurt all over; there was a peculiar heaviness in her right arm and leg.

Blue legs halted beside her as she tried to raise her head. A voice said, "Take it easy, Miss; don't try to move. Be a doctor along to see you any minute."

She closed her eyes and began to identify separate sounds, moans and cries, the throb of engines, the hiss and splash of water against wet, smoldering wood. Memory came back to her in a rush. The fire. Greg. She tried to get up but she couldn't move. She tried to call his name and thought she was calling it until, hazily, it occurred to her that the name she heard being called wasn't Greg's and the voice wasn't her own.

The keening note of a siren drowned it out.

She turned her head slowly. Other people lay on the ground all around her. An ambulance stopped within her range of vision and white-clad men jumped out of it.

"Tommy!" a woman's voice called. "Tommy!"

The girl's eyes found her, a woman with her dress hanging in tatters, one arm bleeding profusely, most of her hair burned off. She moved in a daze among the prone figures, calling Tommy. The girl wondered vaguely why Tommy didn't answer.

Tirelessly, the woman wandered and called.

Two firemen came out of the hotel, carrying a bundle wrapped in a tarpaulin.

Somewhere a child wailed a terrified protest against such a world as this had become.

The fire had been brought under control. The living and the dead were being carried out steadily now.

The girl heard a man weeping, talking to anyone, no one, saying, "Look, he's dead. He's dead but he's still got his dog. Look, he's still got it. He's dead, he's dead as can be but he never let go of his dog."

Ambulances, trucks commandeered as ambulances and hearses, doctors, more police officers and firemen, all were arriving in increasing numbers to take charge and do what they could among the horrors that confronted them. No one listened to the man who wept so helplessly. No one but the girl. He had stopped near her. She listened and then looked at him, her glance moving up his legs to the little boy dead in his arms and, somehow, even in death, still clutching the polka-dot dog.

She screamed, a long immemorial cry of anguish, and tried frantically to get to her feet. Pain such as she had never known washed her away on a wave of blackness.

When next she opened her eyes she found herself on a bed in a long corridor filled with other beds where people groaned or whimpered or lay still in drugged sleep. She faced a window. It was dusk outside. Dim lights burned in the corridor. Two nurses stood in a doorway, holding a low-voiced conversation.

The girl's arm, in a cast to the shoulder, was a dead weight against her side. Her leg hung suspended over the bed in a metal frame.

This time no merciful haze gave her a respite from reality. She remembered instantly what had happened—the fire, the little boy swept away from her, his body in the man's arms.

She began to sob uncontrollably.

A doctor and a nurse appeared beside her.

"This won't do," the doctor said gently. He had a kind face and eyes that commiserated as if they hadn't looked into every depth of suffering since the fire, as if hers was something rare with a quality all its own.

"We'll give you something to make you sleep and tomorrow you'll feel better," he said. "Will you tell me your name and where you live?"

Drowning in tears, she gave him her name and address.

His fingers sought her pulse. He said something in an aside to the nurse and then brought his attention back to her. "Is there someone you want to ask about? Someone who was at the fair with you?"

She shook her head. "No," she said. "I was alone."

Chapter One

On the last Monday of September, 1958, Andrea Langdon awoke at five minutes of eight. She had gone to bed early the night before, after a heavy weekend schedule of playing political hostess for her father, but now, with nearly ten hours' sleep behind her, she felt rested and, even in the moment of awakening, looked nowhere near her twenty-eighth birthday, due in January. An exquisite complexion, dazzlingly fair, was mainly responsible for this. Her eyes, gentle blue eyes under winged brows darker than her pale brown hair, had an older look, a graveness, a shadow of somberness, and in repose her face had something of the same expression.

Her glance wandered over her room with its soft rose and ivory décor and settled on the open window opposite her bed, through which the sun slanted in to announce that this was to be a beautiful early autumn day.

A busy one, too, Andrea reflected, stretching until she was wide awake. Hair appointment at eleven, for one thing. Should she let Pierre try something new with her hair as he'd wanted to last time? No. She preferred it as it was, straight fringe in front, French twist in back. When she was ready for something different, it must be her decision, not Pierre's, even though he was Ridgeway's leading hairdresser, catering at elite prices to the elite of that lower Connecticut city and its suburbs.

Eight o'clock. She tossed back the percale sheet and light cashmere blanket, smoothed down her silk nightshirt, and got out of bed to walk barefooted across the deep-piled ivory rug and polished bare floor to the window.

She looked out on wide clipped lawn and hedge, a segment of big white barn and paddock fence; on beds of dahlias, chrysanthemums, and late roses of every color and kind; on meadows and woods and hills; on distant rooftops of High Point Village, ostentatiously rural, with a millionaire's estate at every crossroads.

She had been living at Hopewell Farm for over three years, but she still had moments of being startled at looking out on open country instead of the house next door in Littleton. Littleton was a city near the New York State line, and, even though Andrea's old home there was situated in a neighborhood of palatial houses and grounds, still, it was a city street. Hopewell Farm was, for

26

all its well-tended, moneyed look of a gentleman farmer's estate, a far cry from the urban setting of Littleton. Her father had bought it when he retired from the presidency of Grocery Mart, a chain of food markets.

Andrea, who had begun by teasing him about changing her name to Maud Muller, had grown to love it through all its varying seasons and moods—the long walks and horseback trails it offered, the joys of gardening under the tutelage of black Sam, the quiet tempo of its days, the new closeness to her father, who was learning dairy farming from the man who ran the farm. Ridgeway was near at hand when she wanted a change, but she had become more and more content to spend her time at Hopewell Farm. She was happier than she had been in many years.

In spite of his interest in the farm, Andrew Langdon, after his retirement, hadn't given his full time to it for very long. Only sixty when he decided to retire, it couldn't begin to take up the energies of a man of his ability and background. Ridgeway was only ten miles away and he had long held directorships in a number of its banks and industries and had a wide acquaintance there. He soon found himself in demand to take part in its ambitious regional program for the whole area. Two years ago he had accepted the chairmanship of the Metropolitan Redevelopment Commission. This had brought him into politics. And now, for the first time, he was running for office.

Andrea was very proud of her handsome, white-haired father. She couldn't imagine how he had avoided remarriage in the twenty years since her mother's death. There had been, certainly, enough women who had tried to marry so eligible a widower. But he wasn't to be captured. Whatever love interests he might have had, not bound for the altar, had been managed so discreetly that Andrea knew nothing about them.

This late September morning, standing at the window she thought about her father with maternal concern. She must be sure to remind him just before the TV men arrived tonight that he mustn't, while in front of the camera, run his fingers through his hair or pull at his lower lip as was his habit. He must be the dignified statesman type through the whole half hour of *Program Personality*. Voters would be watching it and must not find one tiny mannerism, however endearingly familiar she found it herself, to criticize.

She smiled a little, thinking of her father, and then became serious again. Tonight was serious for her father. *Program Personality* wasn't a paid political program on a local station. It was a weekly public-service feature seen throughout the whole state. Her father had been invited to appear on it because of his work as chairman of the Redevelopment Commission. It was on this project that he would talk tonight, but his appearance had larger implications.

Andrew Langdon was running for Congress. He had been nominated at the Republican Convention last summer for the seat being vacated in the Sixth Connecticut District, a safe Republican district since time out of mind. And not only had he, a political novice, won this important nomination but beyond the congressional Alps lay the governorship. He was regarded as such an ideal candidate that already he was being talked of in high Republican circles as gubernatorial timber. Tonight marked his first state-wide television introduction to the people of Connecticut.

Andrea's thoughts turned to the living-room draperies. The cleaner had promised to deliver them the first thing this morning. If they weren't here by the time she was ready to leave for the hairdresser's she must be sure to call and ask what the delay was. And tell Hilda to have Sam hang them. Oh, and while Sam was available, have him cut quantities of flowers for tonight. He could leave them in the sink in the butler's pantry and Andrea would arrange them as soon as she was back from the hairdresser's. Simple homey arrangements, she reflected wryly. Nothing that smacked of the florist's arts, nothing that the feminine voter might consider uppity.

She would do the flowers after lunch. At three o'clock the *Ridgeway Post* was sending a woman reporter to interview her for the Sunday woman's page, not on the grounds of personal achievement but as her father's daughter. At five-thirty or so she'd have to look in on Betsy's cocktail party for the visiting cousin from Cleveland; then there'd be early dinner in order to be ready for *Program Personality* at eight. She must be sure to check again with Mrs. Callum on the refreshments, solid, for the cameramen, interviewer, and friends who would drop in later; and with her father on refreshments, liquid.

Five minutes past eight. Breakfast was at eight-thirty, with Mrs. Callum feeling put upon if one were late. Andrea hurried into her bathroom and turned on the shower.

At 8 P.M. on that last Monday of September, in a waterfront bar in New London, Connecticut, well and unfavorably known to the police, Seymour Boyd rested an elbow on the stained, dilapidated bar and stared morosely into his almost empty glass. Through many years and many vicissitudes he had drifted, always downward, from a fine home in his native North Carolina to this dubious spot. In his pocket were thirty-two dollars, all that was left out of fifty won in a card game last night and all that stood between him and destitution. On his back was his only suit of clothes, shiny with age, threadbare and soiled. On his still handsome face—he was only thirty-five—was the stamp of dissipation and moral decay. He was six feet tall, redheaded, gaunt from weeks of being on a drunk without proper food or lodging. His last job had been in Hagerstown, Maryland. He had walked out on it with twenty-three dollars in his pocket the third week of August. The time since then, like many times before it, was more or less a blur. He couldn't have figured out, if he had wanted to, what had brought him to New London or how he had got there. He knew no one in this part of the country, usually heading South or West rather than North in his wanderings. But here he was in New London and he might as well stay for a while. There were plenty of sailors around to drink with and pluck in card games.

The television set above the bar was turned on. To Seymour it was nothing more than voices and music in the background, to which he paid no attention. Presently a commercial came on and then a new voice, professionally rich and well modulated, announced that this was *Program Personality* and tonight's guest would be Mr. Andrew Langdon.

Langdon. The name caught Seymour Boyd's attention. Once, years ago—He turned an indifferent glance on the screen.

Former resident of Littleton, the announcer said. Retired president of Grocery Mart. Civic leader. Chairman of the Ridgeway Metropolitan Redevelopment Commission.

Andrew Langdon, the man at the bar ruminated. Andrea Langdon. Washington. Miss Merrivale's School for Girls.

"Mr. Langdon's present home is Hopewell

Farm in High Point Village near Ridgeway. Mr. Langdon will discuss his work on the Redevelopment Commission, and perhaps he'll digress a little to tell us something of his experiences as a newcomer to dairy farming. We take you now to Hopewell Farm . . ."

The bar was nearly empty. But from one of the few occupied booths a man called, "Hey, get something else."

The bartender, pouring another drink for Seymour, said, "Okay, just keep your shirt on."

Seymour stared at the white-haired man seated in an armchair in a beautiful paneled room, while nearby on a Hepplewhite sofa —

". . . his daughter, Miss Andrea Langdon, her father's hostess, adviser, consultant — what else, Miss Langdon?"

Andrea. After all these years. Andrea.

"Keeper," Andrew Langdon interjected lightly. "Yes indeed." He was very much at ease, secure within himself and in his position in life. "Watches my diet, tells me what time to go to bed, what time to get up, what tie doesn't go with what suit — "

"Father, it's a well-known fact that far more men than women are color-blind," Andrea commented demurely.

Her father and the interviewer laughed. The bartender reached up to change the station.

"Leave it on," Seymour said.

"But those guys in the booth — "

"Leave it on, I said." Seymour's soft voice hardened and his coppery-brown eyes challenged the bartender truculently.

The latter, who spent his working hours trying, not always with success, to avoid trouble, left the program on, turning a deaf ear to the complaints from the booth.

Andrew Langdon answered questions and talked about the work of the Redevelopment Commission. He was serious and thoughtful, without a trace of the pompous. Whenever the camera picked up Andrea, it revealed her sitting quietly on the sofa, her full-skirted dress spread gracefully around her, her eyes under their lovely winged brows fixed attentively on her father.

Andrea. Seymour did arithmetic in his head. Why, it was nearly ten years ago. And she was still Miss Langdon. Langdon Grocery Mart, they said. God, her old man must be rolling in money! Look at him, look at the room, the whole setup. It stank of money. If he'd known about Grocery Mart ten years ago — But she hadn't said a word. The school she'd attended had told him, of course, that there was some money in back of her. But he just hadn't thought it out. A chain of supermarkets! He'd seen one of them today, the parking lot crowded with cars. If he'd only known ten years ago —

And look at Andrea herself. Poised, serene, she was a beautiful thing. Why hadn't she married?

33

Maybe she had been married and got a divorce and resumed her maiden name.

What about the kid she was going to have?

She'd got rid of it. Why not? She was in a position to hire the best abortionist in the country.

Christ above, what a fool he'd been!

Seymour drained his glass. No use thinking of it now. It was too late. Or—was it?

At 8:10 P.M. on that last Monday of September, Effie Horbal put away her ironing and went into the sitting room of the Oldfield farmhouse. Her husband, Walt, had just finished reading the evening paper. He dropped it on the floor and said, "Whyn't you see what's on television?"

Effie turned on the set, flicked it past a newscast to the next channel, and almost flicked it past that. A man was talking, a fine-looking older man. Then, in the split second before she would have turned the knob again, the camera shifted to a young woman seated on a sofa.

Effie caught her breath. "Walt, look! Isn't that—it looks like Miss Lambert!"

"It is her," he said. "What's she doing on television?"

Effie sat down on the nearest chair. The camera went back to Andrew Langdon. He laughed at something the interviewer said—the Horbals missed it—and replied, "Well, I must confess that

34

my role of farmer is pretty much nonexistent at the moment. As you may have heard—"

The interviewer laughed. "Yes, Mr. Langdon, I believe it has come to my attention that you're running for Congress this year in the Sixth District . . . What do you think of your father going into politics, Miss Langdon?"

The camera picked up Andrea again, smiling at her father. "I'm very much pleased, of course," she said.

"I'm going to see to it that she works as hard as I do during the campaign," Andrew Langdon said, smiling back at her.

Effie said, "Walt, they're calling her Miss Langdon!"

"Sure they are." He lit a cigarette and gave his wife a cynical glance. "I told you all along the name she gave us was phony. I wonder where the kid is now? I bet you won't hear a word about him on this program."

The camera went back to Andrew Langdon. He talked about regional planning, water and zoning needs and highway problems related to it.

Walt Horbal sat back in his chair. "What d'you know," he said. "Her old man's loaded, that's for sure. I wonder where the kid is? How old is he now?"

Effie counted back. "It was just a couple of weeks before his fifth birthday that Miss Lambert—"

"Langdon."

"Well, Langdon, then. It's four years ago she took him away, so now he's almost nine. His birthday's October 7. That's next week."

"Zatso?" Walt Horbal eyed her thoughtfully. "And he's got a grandfather running for Congress and crawling with money. Maybe we ought to send the kid a birthday present, huh?"

He was a big burly man with a deceptive surface heartiness but mean eyes and a mean mouth. His wife, small and thin and as kind as he would allow her to be, gave him a startled glance. "But when she took him away, Miss Lambert said she wanted to make it a clean break. We agreed it was best. So how can we send Greg a present? We don't know the address; we're not even supposed to know her real name."

"When she's on TV does she expect to keep it a secret?"

"But Walt, I guess she thinks we're away off in Nevada. We told her we were going to stay there for good, you know."

Walt thought his wife was reminding him that he'd let her inheritance from her aunt run through his fingers in Las Vegas, where his luck had been uniformly lousy. He was touchy on the subject. He snarled, "The hell with what Miss Lambert-Langdon thinks about us. If she ever thinks about us at all, which I doubt. You buy the kid a present and I'll get hold of a Ridgeway telephone directory and find out where to send it, care of Miss Andrea Langdon." He grinned knowingly. "Happy birthday to Greg from his old friends, the Horbals."

Effie was silent. She'd have to do what Walt said; he'd keep after her until she did, but she didn't have to approve of it. She sighed.

His mean look was gone for the moment. "I bet she's got the kid tucked away in some swank school," he said.

Effie thought about the little redheaded boy with his shy dignity, his sudden bursts of affection. She would have liked to have kept Greg. He'd have been company, someone to love.

It had been years since she had felt love for her husband. Looking at him now, it didn't seem possible that there'd ever been a time when she had loved him.

"Crawling with money," he said, looking at Andrew Langdon on the screen and savoring the golden possibilities the phrase conjured up.

At eight-fifteen that last Monday of September, Fergus MacDonald, political writer for the *Ridgeway Post,* drifted into Ridgeway County Republican Headquarters in a suite in the Wilton Hotel. He found an assembly of the faithful, including Chuck Grennan, county chairman, gathered around a TV set watching *Program Personality.* Chuck Grennan took his eyes off the screen to say, "Hi, Fergus," and gesture hospitably toward a table where drinks were set up.

Fergus mixed himself a scotch and soda, sat down, and, rather in the manner of a cattle buyer looking over beef on the hoof, turned an appraising eye on GOP wares in the person of Andrew Langdon.

The campaign had just begun to warm up; the only time Fergus had met the candidate had been at the convention where Langdon, hand-picked by the state central committee, had been nominated without opposition. Fergus was congenitally suspicious of hand-picked candidates, but as he watched *Program Personality* he thought that his original favorable impression of Andrew Langdon had been sound.

When the camera switched to Andrea, he said, "Well," under his breath and a moment later to Chuck Grennan, "Why didn't you pick her? Lots prettier, lots more sex appeal than her old man."

"Oh I don't know," the county chairman replied. "How many widows between forty and sixty are there in the Sixth District? They'll go for Langdon. We're not keeping it a secret that he's a widower."

Fergus grinned and was silent again, watching Andrea, admiring not only her looks but her poise and unaffected simplicity. The program was almost over; the camera focused on Andrea. She smiled. She had a lovely slow smile, Fergus thought.

She was enchanting. Why on earth wasn't she married, a girl like her with so much to offer in herself and with social position and money thrown in for good measure?

The camera shifted back to her father. He said he'd very much enjoyed being on the program. The interviewer said he'd enjoyed it, too, and it came to a close on this note of mutual felicitation.

There was a burst of admiring comment and a general move toward the bar among the group at GOP headquarters.

"Pretty good, huh?" Chuck Grennan said.

"Wonderful," Fergus replied, almost dreamily.

The county chairman looked a little startled— Fergus wasn't given to unqualified praise—and went on, "He's a natural. I knew it as soon as I met him last year. Had to sell him to the committee, of course—a novice, a babe in the woods, politically. But he's got everything: background, money, good appearance, a fine business reputation, real progressive type, too, no labor troubles; wouldn't be a bit surprised if he pulled some of the labor vote." Chuck paused. "Daughter'll be an asset. We'll have to see to it that she's on the platform with him every time he makes a speech."

Fergus finished his drink and looked at the older man from under black brows. He said, "All you've got in your veins are registration figures. Not a drop of red male blood."

Chuck laughed. "Got me a nice wife at home. I've stopped looking."

"When you stop looking you're dead."

"Oh well . . ." Chuck got to his feet. "Guess I'll take a run out and congratulate him. Except for Fairfield County, Langdon's about the only shoo-in we've got in the whole state this year. Off the record, of course," he appended hastily.

"Of course," Fergus agreed. "But I'm beginning to wonder if you've got a shoo-in anywhere. Including Fairfield and Ridgeway counties." He rolled his *r*s a little. He had been born in Scotland and although his parents had migrated to the United States when he was four he had never quite lost the burr in his speech.

"Come off it," Chuck said. "We'll run scared everywhere because that's our best bet. But the Sixth District—for God's sake, only Democrat ever got elected was when you were still sucking on a bottle back in '36 in the Roosevelt landslide."

"In 1936 I was eleven years old. Too old for a bottle of milk, too young for a bottle of scotch."

"All right, so you remember the '36 election. Good thing you do. Only time a Democrat got elected from Ridgeway County."

"Ah," said Fergus. "You better start reading my dope stories. Within the next couple of days I'll publish the MacDonald poll's preliminary soundings on the Sixth-District seat."

Chuck frowned. "If Langdon isn't out in front by a country mile, you're dreaming. Look, you want to go out to his place with me? Give you a chance to get acquainted with him. Might be useful," he added casually, "if you get around to doing a personality sketch on him or something."

Fergus laughed. "You're so subtle, Chuck. I don't know where Langdon lives. I'll follow you in my car."

They went out of the room together, the chunky, affable county chairman, the tall newspaperman, a black Scot, black-haired, black-browed, dark of skin, with light gray eyes that looked lighter than they were in his dark face. He got into his Volkswagen—though unmarried and earning a good salary he did not throw his money around on fancy cars—and followed Chuck Grennan to Hopewell Farm.

Lights shone from nearly every window of the big brick house, and several cars were parked in the half-moon driveway in front.

"Looks like open house," Chuck remarked, as they went up the front steps. "Of course Langdon can afford to treat his friends to the best there is. Nice place he's got."

A minute later they were inside shaking hands with Andrew Langdon, who came to the living-room doorway to greet them. He said smilingly to Fergus, "My daughter will want to meet you, Mr. MacDonald. Since she's become interested in politics she's a faithful reader of your column."

He beckoned to Andrea, who was the center of a younger group across the room. As she came toward them, it crossed Fergus's mind that her blue dress, beautifully made and fitted, must have cost at least his week's salary. Then he wondered why such a thought had even occurred to him. Andrew Langdon's daughter was in a different world.

What a peach-bloom complexion she had. Television hadn't shown that.

She held out her hand and gave him her lovely smile. "How do you do, Mr. MacDonald. I read you every day."

He took her hand. He forgot whose daughter she was and how far it put her out of his reach.

Chapter Two

It was the following Thursday. Fergus had asked Andrea to have dinner with him the night they met. She had seemed pleased to accept his invitation and now she seemed to enjoy his company.

"Just the usual sort of thing," Fergus said, smiling at her across the table. "High-school paper, college paper, then like a homing pigeon to the *Post* where I'd had a job a couple of summer vacations. So you see," he quirked an eyebrow at her, "it's all very routine."

"It doesn't seem routine to me," she said. "I think most people are interested in newspaper work."

"Oh yes. They feel it has glamour."

"I suppose so." She smiled.

He looked at her, elegant in black, wearing pearls, the light above the table bringing out the delicate bloom of her skin, the curve of her mouth sensitive and a little sad.

He went on looking at her. Her smile erased the shadow and gave her face a vivid look. It was years, he reflected, since he'd met a girl to whom he felt as instantaneously and strongly attracted as he did to Andrea.

But she was Langdon's daughter. The big house, the real pearls, the chain of supermarkets representing God knew how much, the air of breeding, the patrician look—how did he fit in with all that? He was Fergus MacDonald, son of Scottish immigrant parents, thrifty, hard-working people of no particular background who had made many sacrifices to educate their sons. Both parents were dead now. Their estate, shared with his brother Jim in California, had come to just over five thousand dollars. Andrea Langdon would inherit how much? Five hundred thousand? Five million? He had no idea. He only knew that it depressed him to think of the barrier her money made between them.

Then he gave himself a mental shake. He mustn't get a thing about it. Hadn't he lived long enough to know you had to take each day as it came?

"What did you do when you first went to work for the *Post?*" she asked.

"What did I do? Woman, I dinna remember all the fearful details twelve years later. I started in as a trainee. By grit and perseverance, plus natural brilliance, of course, I became a police reporter, took on general assignments, and then they thought I showed a flair for political writing. So here I am."

"You must like it," she said. "You couldn't do it so well if your heart wasn't in it."

His brows came together in a mock frown. "Lesson number one in politics is that you keep your heart out of it or you'll land on another portion of your anatomy."

She laughed but protested, "Father wouldn't agree with that. He's one of the kindest people I've ever known. And it's not just because he's my father either."

"I'll accept it." Fergus paused. "Having met his daughter."

He spoke lightly to keep it from sounding too banal. Her reaction surprised him. A guarded look came to her face.

Good Lord, he thought, doesn't she like compliments? Why not?

She said, "You mentioned Father in connection with the governorship in a story you wrote last week. Other newspapers have, too. It bothers him. He thinks it's premature since he has no experience at all in politics."

"He won't be able to say that on November 4," Fergus commented. "He'll have learned a lot by that time. And in the meantime people are taking notice of him. He's a political natural, Miss Langdon—Andrea, if I may."

"Yes."

"Every so often one comes along," Fergus continued. "A man who has everything as a candidate — appearance, background, intelligence, no messy interludes to be explained away or hushed up, and above all, common sense. I should have put common sense first," he added after a moment's thought. "It's a pearl beyond price in politics. Our present governor has plenty of it, just plain common sense that keeps him on balance, keeps him from getting out on limbs that can be sawed out from under him. In this state we value it enormously. We're not called the land of steady habits for nothing. If your father's elected, people will find out he has the same qualities the governor has, including the enormous asset of common sense."

"If he's elected?" Andrea looked at him in astonishment. "But in the Sixth District —"

"I know. Safe sure Republican district. But there's always the chance it might turn out to be a Republican Jericho this year. The Democratic trumpet's blowing hard."

"Mr. Grennan wouldn't agree with you. He says —"

"Well, would you expect Mr. Macy to say Mr. Gimbel's going to outsell him this year?"

"Oh." She sighed. "I don't see how I can bear it for Father if he doesn't win. But I suppose Mrs. Chapman feels the same way about her husband and there's only one Sixth-District seat. Isn't it too bad someone's always got to lose?

Think how wonderful it would be if everyone could win." She laughed at herself ruefully as she spoke.

"No poverty, no sin, no sorrow either, I suppose, in this utopia of yours?"

"None at all."

She was suddenly so serious that he remarked, "But we're talking now about things very far away from your life. That was my first impression of you on TV the other night, you know; someone untouched by ugliness of any sort."

She gave him a quick glance. "I'm twenty-seven years old, Mr. MacDonald —"

"Fergus."

"Fergus. I wasn't born with a guarantee that I'd escape the unpleasant side of life. I've escaped poverty, yes, but when I did volunteer social work a few years ago I at least found out what it was like, the terrible things it does to people."

"And did whatever you could to alleviate it, I'll bet," he inserted.

"Well, I tried. But sometimes it seemed there wasn't enough money in the world to alleviate the kind of poverty I ran into. As for the other things, sin and sorrow, you said, I'm no more immune to them than anyone else."

"No?" Looking at her, he couldn't take what she said very seriously. She didn't know what real sin and sorrow meant, he thought. He hoped they would never touch her; if he had his way he would like to be able to shield her from them himself.

The faint shadow was back on her face just then as if her thoughts were far away. He didn't want that; he wanted her full attention given to him.

The waiter served dessert and made a ceremony of bringing on a silver coffee service. When he had bowed himself off, Fergus asked, "What sort of volunteer work did you do, Andrea? Junior League?"

She thought she detected dryness in his tone and pointed out that League membership required a certain number of hours in accredited agencies. She had worked mostly at St. Margaret's, an Episcopal orphanage.

"Do you do the same sort of thing now at the children's home in Ridgeway?" he asked.

Andrea shook her head and told him she did some volunteer work at the hospital but that was all. Then she changed the subject with a question about politics.

Fergus answered it and brought the conversation right back to her. He wanted to know much more about her. Andrea, though, was reluctant to talk about herself. She offered him the merest sketch: her mother's death when she was seven, her great-aunt presiding over the house in Littleton until she died when Andrea was thirteen, then Miss Merrivale's in Washington, junior college. Since her father's retirement they had done some traveling, but most of their time was spent

48

at Hopewell Farm. She liked doing things with her father, she added; she had missed him a lot when she was younger and business kept him away from home so much of the time.

Fergus watched her as she talked. She was just about the loveliest thing he'd ever seen, he thought. He shook his head at himself. The older they are the harder they fall—did that apply to him? Well, he thought next, subconsciously, perhaps he was ready for marriage now and hadn't realized it. But Andrea, no matter how right she seemed for him in other ways, had too much money.

Why wasn't she married herself? There must be a very good reason . . .the question was, what could it be?

Suddenly, without intending to, Fergus asked her what the reason was.

Her face turned pink. "I might ask you the same question," she countered.

"The answer's a lot of things." He eyed her forthrightly. "I came closest to it eight or nine years ago, but while I waited and wondered if we could get by on what I earned at the time, the girl got engaged to someone else. Then, with my job involving a lot of odd hours and one thing or another, I just didn't get serious about any particular girl." He paused. "I guess the truth is, the longer you put it off the harder it is to make up your mind. You develop a crust of self-sufficiency, self-centeredness or whatever. Not," he hastened to add, "that we're in the same age bracket or anything like it, but still, I'd expect you to have been grabbed off long ago."

"Well, it's just one of those things. Let's leave it at that." She smiled to soften her reply.

Which wasn't a reply at all, Fergus reflected, but an evasion, a refusal to answer a question he shouldn't have asked in the first place. And what difference did it make to him anyway? The best thing he could do about her, a girl out of his reach, was to take her home and forget he'd ever met her.

He knew he would do no such thing.

Chapter Three

Saturday afternoon, two days after her dinner date with Fergus, Andrea sat in the library making out a mailing list for her father's use in the campaign. Although the door stood open on the hall, she was so absorbed in what she was doing that when the front doorbell rang she scarcely heard it or Hilda's footsteps answering it and didn't look up until Hilda came into the room and said, on a doubtful note, "Miss Langdon, there's a—"

"Gentleman to see you," a voice broke in from behind the maid, a soft drawling voice Andrea thought she had forgotten and had never expected to hear again.

Seymour Boyd hadn't waited near the front door where Hilda, after a glance that took in his seedy appearance, had left him. He had followed her along the hall and stood in the doorway.

Andrea dropped her pen on the desk and got slowly to her feet, her face pale with shock, her eyes disbelieving what they saw.

He brushed past the maid, his hand outstretched. "It's wonderful to see you again, Andrea. Wonderful!"

She couldn't find her voice immediately. She let him clasp her hand in both of his. This close to him she smelled liquor on his breath.

Hilda lingered uncertainly until Andrea said in dismissal, "Thank you, Hilda."

The maid went away. Andrea freed her hand from a physical contact detestable to her. She moved back a few steps and went on staring at him. This was Seymour, older, his face lined with dissipation, remembered coppery-brown eyes set in circles of puffy flesh, the rest of his face, the features sharpened, thin to the point of gauntness. He looked like a fox, she thought. She had never noticed it years ago but that was what he looked like. Reynard the fox.

"I haven't done justice to you in my memory, Andrea." His eyes and his voice caressed her. "You're even lovelier than I remembered. Much lovelier."

"Why did you come here?"

"Why, Andrea—" tone and glance reproached her. "I was passing through Ridgeway—"

Passing through. She dared to breathe again. Just passing through.

52

"Old times' sake," Seymour continued. "Felt I must stop by and say hello."

Passing through.

"Can't we sit down?" he said. His voice fell faintly on her ears, drowned out by her own inner voice saying over and over, passing through, he isn't staying around here, he'll be gone in a few minutes.

"I don't have a car," he said. "I took a bus to High Point and walked over. It's a bit of a hike, so if you'll sit down, Andrea, I'll be happy to occupy one of these comfortable-looking chairs myself."

She remembered his smile. It lived on unchanged in the ruin of his face. She had once thought it charming.

She sat down in the desk chair.

Seymour sat down in one of the big leather chairs and stretched out, making himself at home.

"Well," he said, "just fancy seeing you again after all these years."

"How did you find me?"

"It wasn't hard to do. I saw you on television the other night and it brought back so much to me that I felt I had to see you again."

He could say that to her and look at her with what was supposed to be tenderness.

Anger steadied her. "I can't think why."

"Oh come now, Andrea. Please don't take

that attitude. It's all past and done now. A little chat and perhaps a drink, since the walk from High Point left me thirsty. Then I'll leave."

Giving him a drink connoted hospitality, friendliness. She wanted to refuse, but even more she wanted him to go. If she gave him a drink, he would have no excuse to stay after he had finished it.

She went to the built-in bar, mixed him the bourbon and soda he requested.

As he stood up to take it from her he said, "So your father's running for Congress."

"Yes." She went back to the desk chair, putting the width of the room between them.

"Well, here's success to him." Seymour sat down, raised the glass, and all but emptied it before he removed it from his lips.

Andrea said nothing.

His glance rested on her speculatively. "I was surprised that you were introduced on TV as Miss Langdon. I expected you to be married years ago. You never have been?"

"No."

"Neither have I. Can't say I've ever been in a position to."

How could he say that to her? She felt sick, suffocated from being in the same room with him.

His voice deepened as he said, "I know what

54

you're thinking, Andrea. I've regretted it a thousand times. I couldn't face it, though, when you told me. I panicked and took off for home. Then I was going to write to you—"

"I'd rather not talk about it." Her tone would have annihilated a sensitive man.

He shrugged and tossed off the rest of his drink. "I never go home any more," he said and went on to tell her about his family's lack of understanding of the bad luck he'd always had, the way things had gone against him every time he'd thought he was on the way to getting somewhere in life.

She scarcely listened and didn't look at him at all. His tone had a hollow ring. He was hollow, a hollow man who knew the words that denoted normal feeling but spoke them without comprehension, like someone from another planet. He had nothing inside him but appetites and self-pity. How could she have fallen in love with him, suddenly, recklessly, not once trying to look beneath what was then a handsome façade? Even at eighteen, how could she have?

Shame and self-disgust scorched her. She couldn't bear to stay in the same room with this man another minute. She stood up and said, "I'm afraid I'll have to ask you to go."

"Oh?" He rose, picked up his glass, and moved toward the bar. "If you don't mind, one for the road first."

He mixed himself a double bourbon and soda. She watched him with mingled apprehension and anger. Was she going to have to create a scene to get rid of him?

The doorbell rang. Hilda answered it and then appeared in the doorway with a package. "This just came for you, Miss Langdon."

"Put it here on the desk, Hilda."

The maid put down the package and left. Andrea glanced at it without interest and then froze as she read the return address: Mrs. Walter Horbal, RFD #1, Oldfield, Connecticut.

She looked as if she were seeing a ghost, Seymour Boyd thought.

With visible effort she tore her eyes off the package and turned them to him. "I'm sorry but you'll have to go now."

He moved toward her and asked in a cold, brutal voice, "What became of the kid?"

She was standing beside the desk. She looked at him blankly, not moving, not saying a word.

"Our kid," he said. "The product of a certain New Year's Eve ten years ago. What became of it, Andrea?"

The package lay behind her on the desk. Her thoughts filled with grief and shame, and dread fell into chaos. He waited for an answer.

"There was no child," she said at last. "I had a miscarriage."

He smiled knowingly. "Oh. How fortunate."

She stood like a figure of stone.

He thought about what she'd told him. She'd had an abortion—let her call it a miscarriage if she wanted to—just as he'd known she would. He felt chagrined. If there had been a child, he would have had a real hold over her in a setup that stank of money. As it was—

His glance wandered to the package on the desk that had disturbed Andrea so much. From where he stood he could read the large careful print of the return name and address and, without conscious motive, he memorized them: Mrs. Walter Horbal, RFD #1, Oldfield, Connecticut.

"Well, it seems I'm getting the bum's rush," he said, and then adopting a wry expression, "but the truth is, I don't have a place to go when I leave, Andrea. I'm on the road and very much in a state of financial embarrassment at the moment. I've got the promise of a job in Washington, though, if I can only get there."

Washington, she thought. Three hundred miles or more away. She had cashed a check that morning. Give him every cent of it to get rid of him and pray she never laid eyes on him again.

"I can give you what I have on hand," she said. "It should take you to Washington and tide you over for a day or two."

Her pocketbook was upstairs. She took the package with her when she went up to get it.

While she was gone, Seymour poured himself a straight shot of bourbon, downed it, and stood looking around the handsomely furnished room with bitter discontent. What he'd thrown away ten years ago! If he'd only known—if he'd had any sense—

Andrea came back. She had cashed a check for one hundred dollars that morning and gave it all to him and only wished it was more, enough to take him to the ends of the earth, away from Ridgeway.

"Thanks a lot," he said carelessly and stuffed the money into his pocket without a second glance. "I'll regard it as a loan to be paid back when I make my contacts in Washington and pick up a job."

Andrea knew he hadn't the faintest intention of paying it back. It didn't matter. All that mattered was his going. "Good-by, Seymour," she said.

"Oh come now," he chided her. "Must there be such a note of finality?"

"Yes," she said. "That's the way I want it."

"Andrea darling—" honey-soft voice—"are you still holding it against me after all these years that I ran out on you in Washington? After all, I was pretty young at the time and the whole thing just threw me."

He'd been in his middle twenties, a tall, enchanting redhead with the same soft voice, charm to burn, and nothing inside him. If she lived to be a hundred, how could she forget the day they were to meet in the National Gallery? She had waited two hours for him, listening to the murmur of the fountain, looking at the flowers, the stream of sightseers. At first she had waited expectantly—Seymour would come and they'd make plans to be married—then little by little hope had died, and faith, and a piece of her youth . . . and still she'd waited. . . .

Now Seymour waited, appraising her attitude. He would welcome reproaches, the opening they would give him to try to justify what he had done to her ten years ago. She could think of no greater humiliation than to allow this.

She said, "Will you go, please?"

He started to make an angry retort, checked himself, and bowed with easy grace. "Good-by, Andrea. It's been nice to see you again."

She watched him from the library doorway until he let himself out of the house. Then she hurried upstairs to her room, where the package from the Horbals, another by-product of *Program Personality,* she knew, lay in wait for her. She opened it. Inside the outer wrapping was a box done up in gift paper with a card attached that read, "Happy birthday to Greg from Mr. and Mrs. Horbal."

In the box was a football helmet. Tears blinded Andrea as she took it out and looked at it. She put it back and after a moment, to compose herself, burned the wrappings, card, and ribbon in the fireplace in her sitting room.

The heavy plastic helmet wouldn't burn, but she would have to get rid of it immediately. Her hands shook, picking up the box.

When Seymour Boyd left the house he walked down the driveway, stopped at the first clump of evergreens that would screen him from view, and turned to look back. The big gracious house, old brick walls mellow in the September sunlight, its grounds forming a setting into which it blended perfectly—this was Andrea's home, eloquent of the money in back of her.

He studied it with black envy, cursing himself for all that he had thrown away ten years ago. He'd had no idea of what he was doing at the time; he'd thought only of showing Andrea a clean pair of heels, slack-witted fool that he'd been. . . .

He went on looking at the house, groaning and swearing to himself over a mistake past mending. If he'd only had the sense to marry her, there'd have been the child to give him a hold on her and if he'd fallen short of her standards of what a husband should be, well, she had pride and would have kept whatever problems he presented to herself while he'd have been in clover, yes, ass-high in clover. He'd had it made ten years ago and then he'd thrown it away with both hands.

"Jesus Christ, when I think of it," he groaned. "Jesus Christ . . ."

The front door opened and Andrea came out, carrying a box. Shorn of its wrappings it looked like the one that had come in the mail from Mrs. Walter Horbal, RFD #1 Oldfield, Connecticut. Andrea had turned white as a sheet when she saw it and now here she was, taking it somewhere.

She didn't come down the driveway toward him. She cut across the lawn, took a path through an adjacent meadow, and turned into a lane, walking so fast toward a patch of woodland far in back of the house that she was soon out of sight.

Seymour started after her, holding his pace to a saunter in the meadow but picking up speed as soon as he reached the lane where there was underbrush on both sides to offer cover.

Andrea remained out of sight at first. Then he caught a glimpse of her far ahead, moving at the same rapid pace, indeed, almost running. Staying close to the edge of the lane, ready to drop flat on the ground if she paused or looked back, he followed her, lessening the gap between them.

The lane ran through the wood. Presently Seymour caught the glitter of water ahead, a pond sparkling in the sunlight.

Andrea stopped at the edge of the pond. He dropped back behind a tree and watched her. She took something red and shiny, he couldn't see what, out of the box and threw it into the middle of the pond where it sank with a slight splash. She tore up the cardboard box and threw the pieces into the pond. Then she turned back the way she had come, tears pouring down her face as she went past Seymour hidden behind the tree.

He waited until she was out of sight, waited a little longer, counting slowly to one hundred. Andrea did not return. She would go straight home, he thought, drying her tears on the way.

He went to the edge of the pond, took off his shoes and socks, rolled up his trousers, and waded out. The water was clear but deepened unexpectedly. He could see the red object lying on the bottom but even when he went back to shore for a long stick it remained out of reach.

A blue jay, perched on a stump, began to scold him for displaying the same prying curiosity characteristic of itself.

In the end Seymour had to take off his clothes, swim out, and dive under the water to retrieve the red object and bring it to the surface. Naked, standing shoulder-deep, he looked at it. It was a boy's football helmet. That was what Andrea had made haste to get rid of as soon as she got rid of him.

He went on looking at his find with a thoughtful frown. A boy's football helmet . . . And Andrea, who said she'd had a miscarriage, turned white at the sight of the package it came in.

He threw the helmet back into the pond, waded to shore, dried himself on underwear that belonged in the laundry if not the rag bag, and got dressed. He took his time. He had a lot to think about.

Andrea, at her sitting-room desk, wrote a note to Mrs. Horbal, thanking her for the gift and saying she would forward it to Greg. "Although," she wrote next, "I'm afraid he doesn't remember you too clearly. His mother has him now and I am sure it will seem best to her that the clean break of four years ago should stand. But thank you anyway for your thought of Greg. I hope everything is going along well for you and Mr. Horbal. Sincerely, Andrea—" She hesitated. They had known her as Miss Lambert. But now they knew her real last name. She wrote Langdon in a clear hand, put the note in an envelope, and sealed it. She would mail it right away, get it over with. If it could be got over with, ever.

Her heart was like lead as she went out to

her car.

From a vantage point in the lane Seymour watched her drive off toward the village. Then he set out himself for the bus station a mile away.

Chapter Four

Monday morning, less than forty-eight hours later, Seymour Boyd, clean, neatly dressed, and with a fresh shave and haircut, boarded the earlier of two buses making stops in Oldfield.

Over the weekend he had bought a secondhand gray suit in good condition, new shoes, shirts, and other necessities. He had paid a week's room rent in advance in a cheap hotel; and giving a thought to tomorrow for the first time in years, he had stayed sober. He still had twenty dollars of Andrea's money in his pocket.

The bus deposited him in Oldfield at noon. According to the schedule, he would have to catch the two-o'clock bus back to Ridgeway in order to return that day. But as he stood looking around in front of the gas station where the bus had let him off, he wondered how he was to spend as much as two whole hours in the town — if Oldfield could be called that.

There was the gas station flanked by the town hall on one side and a dingy little diner on the other. There was a line of houses facing the road. Across from him was a general store and post office, a church, a one-man barber shop, another line of houses, one of them with a sign that said "Resident State Policeman" in front of it. It gave Seymour pause, but only for a moment. He hadn't come here today to break the law.

He looked around again. There wasn't, it seemed, anything remotely resembling a bar. Not that he would have taken a drink anyway when he had business to pursue, he assured himself. But still, there wasn't a bar in the town.

Indeed, the general store presented the one likely source of inquiry. He crossed the road and directed his steps toward it.

There were two people in the store, a woman customer and a man in back of the counter waiting on her. They talked about some projected change in the mill rate while he weighed a pound of round steak and took a can of tuna fish and a package of dog biscuits from the shelves. It was all very leisurely, the conversation continuing while he added up the total. The woman paid him and left. Only then did he turn his attention to the newcomer.

Seymour, who had been waiting near the cubbyhole reserved for the United States Mail, went up to the counter and smiled pleasantly.

"I wonder if you can help me," he began.

"Someone's picking me up at the gas station a little later," this, in case the man had seen him getting off the bus across the road, "and I thought I might fill in the time with inquiries about some friends of a friend of mine. Their name is Horbal. I've often heard my friend speak of visiting them here in Oldfield."

"Zatso?" The storekeeper assessed the younger man, his gentlemanly bearing to which the neat gray suit, clean white shirt, and fresh haircut contributed, his well-bred voice and pleasant smile. Overlooked were the marks of dissipation on Seymour's face, the shallow restlessness of his eyes.

"You mean Walt Horbal, I guess," the storekeeper said.

"Yes, that's the name. Lives somewhere out of town a bit, doesn't he?" Seymour put his faith in the RFD address.

"That's right. Lives on a farm that used to belong to his wife's folks. Walt don't do much farming, though."

"How's Mrs. Horbal? The same good cook she used to be?"

The storekeeper looked blank. "Don't know as I ever heard anyone speak in particular about Effie's cooking."

Mrs. Walter Horbal's first name was Effie.

Seymour laughed. "Well, it always tasted good to my friend. But perhaps you've been spoiled by having a good cook for a wife yourself."

"I sure have," the storekeeper agreed genially. He turned his head as a door in the rear opened. "Here she comes now."

His wife, grossly fat as if to bear testimony to her culinary skill, waddled into the room and over to a chair near the plate-glass front where she settled herself, disposing her great hams and rolls of blubber carefully over the broad chair seat.

Her husband said to her, "This gentleman is asking about the Horbals. Seems he has a friend who knows them well."

The woman glanced at Seymour. "You don't say?" She took a tentlike garment—a sweater for herself?—out of a knitting bag and began to knit. "I didn't get your name."

"My name is Clinton." Seymour bowed and gave her a smile.

"Well, Mr. Clinton—" she counted stitches, "we don't see much of the Horbals since they came back from Nevada last spring. Never did see much of them, for that matter. They've traded for years at the supermarket over near the mill in Hotchkissville where Walt works." She consulted her husband. "Don't know as we've seen them more than once since they got back, have we, Charley?"

He nodded. "That's right, mama."

The Horbals had been in Nevada. "How long were they out there?" Seymour asked.

"Close to four years," the woman replied, without looking up from her knitting. "The way I heard it, Effie inherited some nice property in Nevada from an aunt that died and thought they'd get ahead real good out there. But it didn't work out, a-course." The woman shook her head, her three chins jouncing. "Anyone would know it wouldn't with a man like Walt."

"Now, mama," her husband protested. "You got no right to say that. How do you know things didn't work out for them?"

"I know they came back to take up where they left off at Effie's folks' place. Good thing she didn't sell it, else she probably wouldn't have a roof over her head today."

The storekeeper glanced at Seymour and said apologetically, "My wife don't have too good an opinion of Walt."

"He never amounted to a row of beans," the woman said in the tone of one merely stating a fact. "Let that place of Effie's go to seed, never even put in much of a garden after he started working at the mill." She paused. "I'm surprised they took him back. A-course he never had much of a job there anyways."

"Now, mama—"

She paid no attention. "I always liked Effie," she said, addressing the wall at a point midway between Seymour and her husband. "No gumption to her, but she's a well-meaning woman who tries to do her best. I wonder what became of the little boy they were boarding? I asked Effie about him before they left for Nevada and she said she'd written his guardian or whoever the woman was about making plans for him."

Little boy. Seymour, lounging against the post-office window, shifted his position. "My friend mentioned him. Cute little fellow, wasn't he?"

"I guess so. Seems to me he was a redhead. I can't hardly remember him, though. I don't suppose I saw him over two or three times all the years Effie had him. And when they're growing from babies into little boys they change fast."

The little boy was a redhead. His son. Seymour raised an eyebrow inquiringly. "But I should think in a small place like Oldfield—"

"Well, even as a girl, Effie kept to herself; living away out there on the farm, she just got in the habit of it. Walt's the same. They do all their trading in Hotchkissville and they're no church-goers, so what is there to bring them into Old-field? Although I'd go crazy myself, living like that on a dirt road miles away from everyone."

"Gravel road," the storekeeper interpolated.

"All right, gravel. But so isolated."

"The little boy was too young to go to school?" Seymour asked.

"When they had him he was. I never did find out what arrangements was made for him when the Horbals left." The woman dredged deep into her memory. "Seems to me I heard at the time that the woman who was boarding him with them came and took him away with her. I guess

70

Effie found it real hard to give him up. She'd had him since he was a baby and he was about ready to start school. No wonder she got attached to him."

"For all we know, maybe the kid's back with them since they got back from Nevada," the storekeeper suggested.

His wife shook her head, setting her chins to jouncing again. "A-course not. We'd of heard. He's a big boy now. He'd be in school and I'm sure we'd of heard if he was back with them."

Yes, Seymour thought, they'd have heard. Very little that went on in Oldfield or its environs would escape the attention of the fat woman in the chair.

"You going to look up the Horbals?" the storekeeper inquired.

"I'm planning to," Seymour said. "That is, if the man who's picking me up gets here early enough. How do I find their place?"

Before the storekeeper could open his mouth, the wife preempted his masculine right to give directions. "Take your left in front here and follow the road for about three miles to a left turn where the sign says Hotchkissville. Go about half a mile on that road and you'll come to a gravel road on your right—at least my husband says its gravel now, it used to be dirt—and that's where the Horbals live, about a mile in from the Hotchkissville road. There aren't but two or three houses on the whole road. You can't miss their place. Hasn't been painted in twenty years or so, I'd say. Least not the last time I saw it, five or six years ago." She paused and looked at Seymour almost in accusation. "I never could figure out a nice person like Effie marrying Walt Horbal. When he first came here twenty-five years ago, I knew the minute I laid eyes on him that he was never going to amount to anything."

"Well . . ." Seymour, in his role of a friend of a friend of the Horbals, tried to look noncommittal. Then he said, "I suppose I can get lunch at the diner across the road."

"If you take my advice you won't order nothing but boiled eggs," the woman said. "The man who runs it buys his eggs from my brother-in-law so I know they're fresh. I can't say the same for another thing that's served over there."

"Now, mama," her husband protested resignedly.

Seymour thanked them and went across the road to the diner. He didn't flinch at the smell of rancid grease that greeted him when he opened the door; he had become used to it in the eating places he could afford to patronize. He ordered two hamburgers, one at a time, and managed to spend an hour over his lunch, prolonging it at the end with a third cup of coffee and pie with a crust the consistency of cardboard. He talked about the World Series with the owner and the few customers who came in. He didn't mention the Horbals. He had found out all he needed to know for the present from the couple in the store. There was no point in making himself conspicuous by further inquiries.

At two o'clock he boarded the Ridgeway bus in front of the gas station, glancing at the store across the road before he got on. The woman was still in the window. He made a gesture intended to convey bewilderment over not having been picked up by car. Her chins jounced up and down in acceptance of his gesture. He got on, took a seat on the opposite side from her, and a moment later the bus left Oldfield behind.

Back in Ridgeway Seymour studied the HELP WANTED MALE columns of the evening newspaper. Kitchen man was about all he could apply for with his work record. But it didn't matter. The father of Andrea Langdon's son needn't demean himself with menial labor for long.

Chapter Five

"This is Saturday, October 11, Andrea," Fergus said on the telephone. "I haven't seen you since we had dinner together a week ago Thursday. In case you can't count, that's nine days ago."

Andrea couldn't match his light tone. She had been too unhappy all week long; not only had the past been reopened but she felt oppressed by fear of what lay ahead in the future. "I've been quite busy," she said.

"So have I. Even so, I found time to call you three or four times. The last time, the day before yesterday, I left a message for you to call me back. But I haven't heard from you."

"I'm sorry. Just as I started to call you, some people came in and then I didn't quite get around to it again."

Didn't have the heart to get around to it again, Andrea amended to herself. Fergus had made a deep impression on her from the moment they met, but what was the use of it? The night she'd had dinner with him she'd allowed herself to dream a little. Then had come Seymour's visit and the package from the Horbals to point up the fact that it had needed only the one television appearance to strip her of anonymity, destroy the smallest illusion that perhaps, after all, the past needn't remain an incubus from which she could never free herself.

The listless note in her voice made Fergus frown. This didn't sound like the girl who had seemed responsive to him last week. "Well," he said, "now that I've got hold of you at last, when may I see you?"

"Why—" Longing fought hopelessness within her. It would mean so much . . . No, it wouldn't because she couldn't allow it to.

She said, "I don't really know. Tonight Father's having some town committee chairmen in and he'll need me here. Tomorrow there are county people coming to dinner. Then Monday I've promised to address envelopes at headquarters. Tuesday I'll be busy, too, and Wednesday there's the Republican Women's dinner at the Wilton for Father. So you see—"

Fergus felt rebuffed and yet puzzled. There was some undercurrent involved, something more than a polite brush-off. He said, "I expect to go to the dinner but I'd like to see you before that. How about late Monday afternoon? I'm going over east of the river earlier in the day to see how

75

the political wars are shaping up, but I'll be back in time to take you away from addressing envelopes long enough to have a drink with me."

She thought, a drink or two, an hour in the hotel cocktail lounge, why deny herself that small pleasure? Besides, Fergus had written some nice things about her father and shouldn't be repaid with rudeness. It wasn't his fault that she couldn't encourage him as she wanted to; it wasn't his fault that ten years ago she had flung away her future and then piled deceit and wrongdoing one on another to hide what she had done; it wasn't his fault that in Broome's Cove cemetery there was a small grave, number 915, nameless to everyone in the world but her. . . .

She said, "Monday afternoon? That would be very nice."

Fergus shook his head as he hung up. He didn't know what to make of the change in her since last week. But perhaps when he saw her Monday—

At least he was going to see her Monday. There was that much on the credit side.

At about the time Fergus made his phone call to Andrea, Seymour Boyd, freshly showered and shaved and dressed in the gray suit, set out for Oldfield in a jalopy borrowed from a fellow employee at Frankie's Handy Lunchroom where he had been employed as a kitchen man for the

76

past three days.

He drove carefully, observing all rules of the road. He couldn't afford to be stopped by a police officer. He had no driver's license although he'd told the jalopy's owner he had one, and he hadn't been behind a wheel in several years.

A two hours' drive in a northeasterly direction brought him to Oldfield. Madame Defarge, he noted sardonically as he went past the general store, was at her post in the window with her knitting, but he doubted that she saw him. He drove through the town, came to the left turn pointing to Hotchkissville, took it, and slowed down to watch for a gravel road on his right.

It was a narrow road without a street or route marker to identify it. Grass grew in the middle, indicating that it was little used. It led Seymour past untilled fields, a deserted farmhouse beginning to fall in upon itself, and then a tangle of stunted woodland. The speedometer registered a mile and a quarter before he went around a curve and saw the house he sought ahead of him, a mailbox out in front with "Walter Horbal" painted on it in black letters and a car standing in a rutted driveway beside it. He pulled in behind the other car, shut off the motor, and looked around him. Madame Defarge was right, he thought; at least twenty years had passed since the house had last received a coat of paint. There were flowers around it — Mrs. Horbal's work? — but otherwise it had an unkempt look. The lawn showed bare patches and badly needed mowing; the barn and other outbuildings were almost past repair; in fact, the whole place testified to the accuracy of Madame Defarge's verdict on Walt Horbal that he didn't amount to much.

But such a man, Seymour told himself as he got out of the jalopy, would serve his purpose far better than an upright, hard-working pillar of society.

A woman answered his ring at the door. In her middle forties, she was thin and harassed-looking, with an anxious frown fixed permanently between her eyes. But there was kindness in her face and in the half smile of greeting she bestowed upon him. He smiled back at her and asked if Mr. Horbal was home.

"Yes, he's here. Won't you come in?"

The small front hall was spotless and so was the sitting room opening off it to which she took him. The furniture was plain and old-fashioned, but sparkling windows and snowy ruffled curtains emphasized its homey and immaculate appearance. Seymour, left to himself while Mrs. Horbal summoned her husband, thought that Andrea hadn't made such a bad choice, after all, of a foster mother and foster home for their child. But for his purposes he hoped Horbal, the foster father, was going to be a very different cup of tea from his wife.

He came into the room. A little shorter than Seymour, he was much heavier and more powerfully built, with coarse features which a stubble of beard did nothing to improve and small eyes hooded by triangular lids.

He looked at Seymour from under the lids and said with his surface heartiness, "My wife says you want to see me."

"Yes, Mr. Horbal." He held out his hand. "My name is Boyd."

Walt Horbal shook hands. He needed a haircut as well as a shave, Seymour, virtuous in his own rehabilitation, noticed. He was a slovenly fellow, very much in contrast to his neat wife.

"Help yourself to a seat," Walt said and slouched down himself in a Boston rocker.

"Thank you." Seymour sat down in a mood of satisfaction. Horbal was his man, just the type he had hoped for. His soft drawl took on an earnest note as he said, "I came to see you, Mr. Horbal, about a little boy who used to live with you."

"Greg?" The hooded eyes turned sharp.

The boy's name was Greg. "Yes," Seymour said. "Greg."

Walt scratched his unshaven chin. It made a rasping sound. "What's he got to do with you, Mr. — uh — Boyd?"

"He's a relative of mine. I understand he lived with you from babyhood up until about four years ago."

"Yeah." The rasping sound was repeated as Walt scratched his chin again. "Haven't seen him, though, since he left. He was a nice kid. Of course Effie—my wife—took care of him mostly. But he was no trouble to speak of and I didn't mind having him around myself. Let her tell you about him." He raised his voice to a shout. "Effie! C'mere a minute."

Effie appeared in the doorway. Punctilious in such matters, Seymour got to his feet. Walt didn't stir. His hand left his chin to scratch his belly. He said, "This is Mr. Boyd, Effie. He wants to know about Greg."

"Won't you join us, Mrs. Horbal?"

"About Greg?" She came forward into the room. Seymour waited until she was seated before resuming his own seat. He turned his smile on her. "He's related to me, Mrs. Horbal."

"Oh." She studied him, the crease between her eyes deepening. "Why, yes, I can see it now. The red hair and the color of your eyes. His hair was lighter red but it's darkened by this time, hasn't it?"

"I imagine so, although I haven't seen him myself since he was a baby." Seymour sighed. "He was a cute little thing then. How I'd like to see him again. He must be—let's see—"

"He was nine last Tuesday, October 7." Effie shook her head. "It doesn't seem possible it's that long since he was a baby. Where is he living now, Mr. Boyd?"

"I hoped you could tell me that, Mrs. Horbal. His—" he paused delicately, "that is, Miss Langdon—didn't say."

"Until the night we saw her on TV we understood her name was Lambert," Walt Horbal put in.

Effie eyed him in discomfort. "No doubt she had her reasons, Walt."

He laughed meaningfully. "I bet she did."

"Walt, what will this gentleman think? It's none of our business what name she gave us. She paid us well to take care of Greg and was always very nice to us. We've got no business talking about her private affairs to anyone."

Effie was showing more spirit than Seymour had expected from her. Her husband didn't like it. He said coldly, "Shut up, Effie. You're always trying to sound so holy. I get goddamn sick of it."

Effie, red with embarrassment, was silenced.

Walt shifted his glance to Seymour. "How are you related to Greg, Mr. Boyd?"

The latter adopted an ingenuous expression that was not at home on his lined, dissipated face. "If you don't mind, I'd rather not go into that. At least not yet. For the moment, will you just take my word for it that we're closely related?"

I wouldn't take your word for what time of day it was, Walt Horbal reflected, staring at him, unimpressed by his manners or cultured speech, sensing a kinship between them based on a lack of scruples and decent standards of conduct.

He grunted an assent, waiting to see which way

the wind blew, catching already the scent of Langdon money.

Seymour turned to Effie. "You keep in touch with Miss Langdon, don't you, Mrs. Horbal? You know, birthday cards and notes back and forth on how Greg is getting on and that sort of thing?"

She fidgeted, looking at her husband. "Well, Miss Lam—Langdon said when she took Greg away—we were leaving for Nevada at the time—she thought it would be better if it was a clean break."

"It was just about this time four years ago," Walt contributed.

"Four years ago last month," Effie said. "September 25, 1954, she took Greg. She got here about ten o'clock and we left for Nevada as soon as they were gone. I'll always remember the date because it was the same day as the fire at the Broome's Cove Fair. Late that afternoon on the Pennsylvania Turnpike we turned the car radio on and the first reports were coming in. You remember, don't you, Walt?"

He nodded. "You kept worrying about whether anyone you knew was in it. Couldn't wait to get the paper the next morning to read the names of the victims. But then all your bellyaching was for nothing. The paper we got out in the middle of Pennsylvania didn't even have the list."

"At least we've established the main point," Seymour interpolated. "You haven't seen Greg since September 25, 1954. You haven't seen or heard from Miss Langdon either?"

"Well . . ." Effie hesitated. Her glance sought counsel from her husband. He slouched lower in the rocker and said nothing. Let her carry the ball. He couldn't figure out what the deal was himself.

"I suppose you saw Miss Langdon on the television show with her father a couple of weeks ago," Effie continued. "I thought she looked lovely. Then Walt and I got talking about it and he said I should send Greg a birthday present. So I bought him a football helmet and sent it to Miss Langdon. She wrote right back thanking me. She said Greg is with his mother now but she'd send on the helmet. Then she said we'd better let things stay the way they are and not try to bring back the past to Greg. He's almost forgotten us, she said."

Where was the kid? Seymour asked himself. In school somewhere?

"You don't get to see Greg either, Mr. Boyd?" Walt inquired.

"No." With unfeigned sincerity Seymour added, "But I'd like to very much."

He got to his feet. "It's been nice to meet you. I'll have to go back to Miss Langdon and have another talk with her about seeing Greg. And perhaps—" his pause was deliberate, "I'll have occasion to see you again."

"I wouldn't be a bit surprised." Walt spoke

with heavy significance.

Effie looked at them in bewilderment. But there was none in the glance they exchanged. They understood each other perfectly.

When Seymour was gone, she said a little doubtfully, "He seems like a gentleman. Lovely manners."

Walt laughed raucously. "Manners, hell. How dumb can you be, Effie? He's on the make for Langdon money. And there's a good chance that we'll get a cut of it too."

"What do you mean?"

"Wait and see."

Effie's face revealed her dismay. "Oh Walt, I wouldn't want you to do anything to make things unpleasant for Miss Langdon. If she wants us to forget Greg, that's her affair. It wouldn't be right for you to—"

"Chrissake, quit nagging," Walt said in his loudest bullying tone. Then he laughed in high good humor. "All that money and her the only child Langdon's got. Sharing the wealth, that don't hurt, does it, Effie? That's good Christian doctrine." He chucked her under the chin and laughed again uproariously.

Effie shrank from his touch. All of a sudden she felt frightened.

Chapter Six

Ordinarily, Seymour Boyd wouldn't even have glanced at the women's section of the Sunday *Ridgeway Post*. He had bought the paper at a newsstand on his way to noon breakfast. Ahead stretched a long afternoon—Frankie's Handy Lunchroom was closed on Sunday—with nothing to do and no place to go but his dreary dirty hotel room until five o'clock, the Sunday opening hour for Ridgeway bars. Therefore, he took his time over breakfast and the paper and presently came to the ABOUT WOMEN section. On the first page of it Andrea's picture, her name beneath it, immediately caught his eye. In the double column below the headline ran: CANDIDATE'S DAUGHTER ENJOYING FATHER'S FIRST VENTURE INTO POLITICAL ARENA.

The story itself, Andrea's background, only child of Andrew Langdon Republican candidate for Congress in the Sixth District, former president of Grocery Mart, educated at Miss Merrivale's School . . . all this Seymour skimmed quickly and went on skimming through what was said about her social prominence, her duties as her father's hostess at Hopewell Farm, her interest in gardening, her volunteer work at a Ridgeway hospital. Then, in covering her life in Littleton, the article mentioned St. Margaret's, the Episcopal orphanage, and Andrea's close identification with it.

The next sentence gave Seymour pause. It read: *"Miss Langdon's work at St. Margaret's came to an end when she suffered serious injuries in the Broome's Cove Fair fire, the disaster that took eighty-nine lives on September 25, 1954. Soon thereafter . . ."*

September 25, 1954. The day Andrea took Greg.

Seymour read on. Andrea's father had retired from Grocery Mart in December, 1954. He had taken his daughter, still recuperating from her injuries in the fire, on a cruise to South America. On their return he had bought Hopewell Farm.

Seymour skimmed the rest. Andrea had done this and that in Ridgeway. She was very pleased, very proud to have her father running for Congress. She liked politics, enjoyed attending political affairs with her father. She planned to help him all she could during the campaign . . . And so forth and so forth.

Seymour went back to Andrea's injuries in the

fire. No mention of a small boy being with her. Of course not. The impeccable Miss Langdon, heiress to Grocery Mart, wouldn't mention picking up her illegitimate son in Oldfield before she went to the fair.

What time had the fire occurred? Andrea hadn't left Oldfield until ten o'clock that morning, according to Mrs. Horbal. But the kid couldn't have been with her when she got to the fair. Somewhere between Oldfield and Broome's Cove she must have dropped him off at a new foster home or placed him in a boarding school.

Seymour hoped it was a school. That wouldn't be nearly as hard to locate as a foster home. In fact, if it was a foster home, he'd need a private detective to trail Andrea until she led him to it.

He shook his head. He was getting too far ahead of himself. The way to handle this thing, this potential gold mine, was to take it a step at a time.

He gave it thought. The first step was to pay a visit to the office of the *Ridgeway Post* and see what he could find out about the fire in general and, in particular, Andrea's injuries in it.

Seymour waited until five o'clock to appear at the office of the *Post*. By that time staff members were coming in and there was enough activity for him not to attract notice. He asked directions to the library. The youthful attendant on duty in the library suggested that the easiest way to look at the issues covering the Broome's

Cove fire was on microfilm. He seated Seymour in front of a viewer, inserted the film for September 1954, and showed him how to operate the machine, running through the early part of the month quickly and slowing it down before the date of the fire was reached.

The September 26 issue carried the big black headline: 89 PERISH IN BROOME'S COVE FAIR BLAZE.

Almost the entire first page was given to the fire, the lead story, eyewitness accounts of horror and heroism, background material, scenes at the improvised morgue, a list of the dead already identified and of those hospitalized at various hospitals in the area.

Andrea's name was not listed.

The fire had broken out at ten minutes of two.

Seymour turned the handle to the next day's issue. Under the headline, DAUGHTER OF GROCERY CHAIN PRESIDENT AMONG INJURED, the *Post* had run a separate story on Andrea. It read:

Miss Andrea Langdon, 23, daughter of Andrew Langdon of Littleton, president of Grocery Mart, suffered arm and leg fractures and numerous bruises in the Broome's Cove fire. Unconscious when she was removed from the scene of the disaster to Broome's Cove Hospital, Miss Langdon was not immediately identified. She later informed hospital officials of her identity and stated that she had attended the fair alone, stopping by chance on her way home from a visit to friends. Her father, Andrew Langdon, has been at his daughter's bedside since she was identified Friday night, some hours after her removal to the hospital. Although suffering from severe shock as well as her other injuries, Miss Langdon is not on the hospital's critical list.

Seymour went through the last three days of the month, reading everything that had been written on the fire. The day after the fire thirty-eight of the dead had remained unidentified; by the last day of September the list had been cut to fourteen: seven women, five men, a girl about twelve, and a boy of five or six.

A boy of five or six. Greg had been five at the time.

Seymour asked to see the October *Post*. The story went on but with less space devoted to it. By October 1 it had moved back to the inner pages. The October 3 issue in a box on the first page stated that there were still nine fire victims unidentified: five women, three men, and the boy. The next day the unidentified victims were again on the first page with a story and picture on their mass burial, in which a priest, a minister, and a rabbi had participated.

Seymour scanned page after page through the whole month of October. There were no further references to the little boy or the other unidentified dead.

He had been supplied with an ash tray. He lit a cigarette and stared at the blank screen of the viewer. No use going on to November. The story had vanished from the pages of the *Post* by mid-October. What about the first anniversary of the fire, though? There was bound to be some sort of résumé of it and perhaps something about the unidentified victims.

He asked for the September 1955 *Post*.

It carried a lengthy review of the fire, beginning on page one and carried over to a back page. Also on the back page was a separate story under the headline, THREE FIRE VICTIMS STILL UNIDENTIFIED. Among them was the little boy. The others, a man and a woman, had been burned beyond recognition, but the little boy, the story said, had died of suffocation and had suffered no burns at all. A description of him followed. *Red hair*—the words leaped from the page at Seymour—*brown eyes, charcoal gray wool slacks and pullover. Still clutching in death a toy polka-dot dog.*

On September 25, 1956, the second anniversary of the fire, the *Post* carried two pictures of the little boy, now the only unidentified victim, the others having been identified during the past year.

The pictures were clear likenesses, one in profile and the other full view. His face was unmarred. Except for the closed eyes with their tangle of dark lashes there was nothing to indicate that he was dead.

He was a handsome child with a sweet mouth and a firm little chin. Something, a pang of sorrow, regret for what might have been, fleeting but sharp, struck Seymour as he studied the pictures. This was his son, his and Andrea's . . .

She had not come forward to identify him and claim the body. What a spot she'd been in, though!

Presently, when the shock of certainty had passed, Seymour's better feelings passed with it. He read the rest of the story. It told about a sergeant of the Broome's Cove police who, long after he had been taken off the case, was still investigating leads on the dead boy's identity. He had asked that the pictures be published in newspapers in the area and advanced various theories—none of them close to the truth—on why a child who had obviously received good care had never been claimed.

The September 25, 1957 issue of the *Post*, in different words, ran the same story on the Broome's Cove sergeant's efforts to identify the little boy. "Little Sir 915," the paper called him—from the number on his grave—and carried a picture of the sergeant putting flowers on it.

The September 25, 1958 issue had another picture of the sergeant decorating Little Sir 915's grave.

By this time the attendant had become friendly with Seymour and ready to advance his own theory on why the child had never been identified. "Foreigners, the parents were," he said. "Lot of flotsam and jetsam left over from the war, y'know. I figure the parents came into the country illegally and when they found out the kid was dead they clammed up for fear they might get deported or something. The only thing wrong is, they could have brought a suit and collected insurance. Plenty of people did from all the companies mixed up in the deal. That's one angle that doesn't fit in with my theory." He eyed Seymour inquiringly. "I suppose you got your own? Everybody who comes in here to look it up has a different one they want to tell you about."

"I'm the exception then," Seymour informed him. "I'll keep mine to myself."

"Oh." The youthful attendant looked nonplussed. "You writing it up for some detective magazine? There's been three or four written already."

"No, not for a magazine." Seymour smiled, enjoying his own irony. "My thought is to give a talk on it. To a very select audience. An audience of one."

"Oh." The attendant looked more nonplussed than ever.

Seymour thanked him and left.

Chapter Seven

Late Monday afternoon Fergus arrived at Republican headquarters in the Wilton Hotel in downtown Ridgeway. Even this late in the day he found it a beehive of activity, with volunteers buried under mountains of campaign literature, telephones ringing, typewriters clacking, people coming and going with an air of haste and consequence. Presiding over this orderly confusion with his usual enthusiasm was Chuck Grennan, who buttonholed the newspaperman before he had done more than wave to Andrea.

"You been over East?" Chuck wanted to know.

"Yup."

"How's it look to you?"

"Like a Democratic sweep."

"Go to hell," Chuck said genially.

"Well you asked me. Did you read my piece yesterday on Fairfield County? Trouble brewing for you there, too."

"Jesus." Chuck looked at him aggrievedly. "You don't sound like an impartial political writer to me, Fergie boy. You sound like a goddamn public-relations guy for the Democrats."

"I have to call them as I see them, Chuckie boy. And every day it looks more and more like you guys haven't got a prayer."

"Well—" Chuck brightened "No matter what the rest of the state does, the Sixth District is in the bag for us. Look at the candidate we've got this year. I tell you—"

Fergus wasn't listening. His gaze moved past the county chairman to the candidate's daughter, who sat at a table addressing envelopes. Sunlight from a nearby window gilded her pale brown hair and heightened the flawlessness of her complexion.

"—everything," Chuck said. "Makes friends wherever he goes. The Rockefeller type, the new Republican-liberal type. Can't miss getting elected, no matter how much malarkey you print in that paper of yours about Democratic sweeps. Langdon'll do the sweeping in the Sixth. You want to make a real name for yourself as a political forecaster, you forget what the goddamn polls and a lot of chickenhearted jerks calling themselves Republicans tell you about how we're going to get the pants licked off us this year. You string along with what your Uncle Chuck tells you, Fergie boy. I've been in this game since you were wearing diapers and I'm telling you—"

Fergus brought his attention back to the county chairman. "Now Chuck, it's been the hell of a while since I wore diapers," he reminded him amiably. "It's been the hell of a while, too, since anybody tried to make me believe in Santa Claus. Save your horse excrement—see how refined I get in GOP headquarters, what a good influence the upper strata have on me?—for your starry-eyed Volunteers-for-Langdon clubs."

"Now wait a minute, Fergie boy—"

But Fergus turned a cynical smile on him and headed for Andrea.

Twenty minutes later, downstairs in the Terrace Room, sitting over cocktails with her, he tried to find words for the change that had taken place in her since he had seen her last. The faint aloofness that seemed to be a part of her, a veil drawn lightly over innate warmth and gentleness, had become more pronounced; the trace of sadness, the shadow on her face in repose, had deepened.

He didn't know what to make of the change. He studied her, his dark face unreadable as he made conversation about his day across the river, calling it his tour of the eastern provinces. She asked polite questions and smiled politely when he tried to be amusing about the battle of the pot holders versus the coffee hours, symbols of the opposing candidates.

She let him order a second round of drinks but then she told him with polite regret that she had to get home soon. Her father expected to be home early and was bringing along some people for dinner.

He didn't sense rejection of him as a person in her attitude. There was even an agreeable moment or two when she became as aware of him as he could ask. Then she withdrew again into a remote and, he thought, very unhappy world of her own.

Something had happened to her since the night they had dinner together. In less than two weeks the change had taken place. The death of someone she was fond of? No, she would have mentioned a thing like that. What else then? A disrupted love affair? No, that couldn't be it, not only because he didn't want it to be true but because she wouldn't have shown interest in him when they met if she was in love with another man.

He introduced a new topic of conversation. "I liked the story on you yesterday." He didn't add that, like a moonstruck adolescent, he had cut her picture out of the paper and put it away for safekeeping. "Caroline did a nice job on it."

"Several people seemed to think so." Andrea didn't add that her one thought when the paper came was that she would never have given the interview if she had known at the time that the Horbals were back in Oldfield. The *Post,* particularly the Sunday edition, was widely read throughout the state. The possibility that the Horbals might have seen it weighed on her.

"I didn't know before that you were in the Broome's Cove fire," Fergus continued.

"Oh, didn't you?" Her tone closed the door on the matter, but he ignored it and said, "I did some features on it at the time. Then last year a detective magazine asked me to do a story for them on the little boy who was never identified. He's had any number of write-ups, of course. It's a baffling thing, isn't it?"

"Yes." Andrea's fingers tightened on the thin stem of the cocktail glass. She picked it up and finished her drink. Then she said, "I am sorry, Fergus, but I'm afraid I must be going," and got to her feet.

"Well, I'll see you to your car." He paid the check and went out to the hotel parking lot with her. She smiled politely and thanked him for the drinks. Her gloved hand rested briefly in his as she said good-by. Then she drove out of the parking lot and, it seemed, out of his life. This time she had given him the brush-off, no two ways about it.

But Fergus, looking after her, continued to be more puzzled than offended. He had an obstinate streak in him and wasn't going to allow himself to be brushed off. Not right away, at least, not until the earlier image of a responsive Andrea had been erased by this new and distant one; or until he became convinced that there was something about him that put him outside the pale where she was concerned.

So far, he felt, that hadn't happened. She'd just retreated into an unhappy world of her own. Within the last two weeks.

What could have happened to her?

He'd find out. He hadn't been a newspaperman all these years for nothing. He'd uncovered many a hidden story in his time. He would uncover Andrea's and try to help her.

His car was in the hotel parking lot. He gave the ticket to the attendant and while he waited for it he thought about the abruptness with which she had put an end to their cocktail interlude. Because she hadn't wanted to talk about the fire. Hadn't wanted to? That was an understatement. She had run away from mention of it. Or was that an exaggeration?

No, he thought, it wasn't.

Chapter Eight

Seymour's hours at Frankie's Handy Lunch-room ran from six-thirty to three with half an hour off for lunch. That Monday afternoon his fellow employee, the owner of the jalopy, suffering from an outsized hangover, at first was surly in refusing to loan it again. Five dollars eventually changed hands and the jalopy then became available to Seymour.

At three o'clock he went to his hotel, changed into his gray suit, and after two drinks at a convenient bar set out for Oldfield.

The October twilight was setting in by the time he reached the Horbals'. He had taken Walt's measure and built what he was going to say around it. The one doubtful factor was Mrs. Horbal; it would be up to her husband to keep her under control.

The Horbals had just finished dinner when he rang their doorbell. Walt answered it and regarded him without surprise. "I thought maybe you'd be back," he said in greeting and led the way to the sitting room.

They sat down. Walt fixed his hooded gaze on him and waited for him to speak.

"I think Mrs. Horbal should hear what I have to say," Seymour informed him, his tone businesslike, no time wasted on exuding charm.

"She's washing the dishes."

"If you don't mind, I think she should be here."

Walt grunted, then bellowed, "Effie!"

She came in, her hands red and moist from dishwashing. She hadn't removed her apron. There was a world of reserve in her manner as she said, "Good evening, Mr. Boyd."

"How are you, Mrs. Horbal." He stood up to greet her, but the courtesy was perfunctory. His attitude made it plain that this wasn't a social occasion.

Effie sat down; alighted, rather, on the edge of a chair and turned an apprehensive gaze on him.

Seymour sat down facing them. "I've been trying to find out where Greg is," he said. "I'm afraid I have but I keep hoping you can prove I'm wrong." He paused, eying them gravely, savoring the sense of power that their moment of suspense gave him. He let the pause lengthen until Walt stirred in his chair, looking impatient. Then he went on, "I want you both to think back to the day Miss Langdon took Greg away; the day of the Broome's Cove fire, you said, Mrs. Horbal."

"Yes, it was. Like I told you, we were on the Pennsylvania—"

"All right. Going back to that morning. Do you remember what Greg wore?"

"Yes, I remember every little thing about it." Her face softened with remembering. "I was so fond of Greg; it was hard to give him up. Before Miss Lam—Langdon came I gave him his breakfast—only he was too excited to eat much—then I gave him a bath and dressed him in his best dark gray wool slacks and a sweater to match. He looked so nice. I can see him yet, looking back and waving when they drove out of the yard." She sighed. "I did enjoy taking care of him, Mr. Boyd. He was such a good little fellow, a real pleasure to have around."

Seymour's expression became graver still in deference to what he would soon tell them. Walt grunted, "So what about his clothes, Mr. Boyd?"

Seymour's attention remained on Effie. He asked, "Did he have a favorite toy, something that he carried with him that day?"

She hesitated. "Well, he had lots of nice playthings. Seems to me, though, that right about then his favorite was a stuffed dog Miss Langdon had brought him. A polka-dot dog with a real perky expression." Her face cleared. "Yes, that was it. He had it under his arm that morning."

Seymour shook his head slowly. "I was afraid

that was what you were going to tell me . . . Greg is dead. He's buried in the Broome's Cove cemetery."

"Oh no!" Effie cried. "Oh no! What happened to him so sudden? It's only two weeks ago I had the note from Miss—she said—Broome's Cove cemetery?—she said he was with his mother—" Effie's incoherent exclamations ended in a burst of tears. She buried her face in her apron.

Her husband shed none. He waited, never taking his hooded eyes off Seymour and discounting entirely his murmurs of sympathy. Presently he said, "All right, Effie, you've bawled long enough. He wasn't your kid and you haven't laid eyes on him in four years."

"But I had him when he was a baby," Effie sobbed. "Remember how cute he was? I just can't believe—"

"I know," Seymour said soothingly. "It's a great shock."

"All right, Effie, that's enough," her husband said. "aid's been dead four years. It's kind of late in the day to bawl over him."

"Four years?" Her face came out of the apron with her reddened eyes forming circles of astonishment. "What do you mean, Walt? Mr. Boyd said he just—"

"Mr. Boyd said nothing of the kind. Why would he ask what the kid was wearing when he left here four years ago if he'd just died?"

She turned to Seymour who nodded. "That's

right, Mrs. Horbal. Greg died in the Broome's Cove fire the day he left here. He's the unidentified child the *Ridgeway Post* calls 'Little Sir 915'."

"Dear God above," she gasped. "I've heard about that child—but we don't get the *Post* and I never dreamed—and then Miss Langdon wrote—"

"Shut up, Effie, and give Mr. Boyd a chance to tell us what it's all about," Walt said.

Seymour had clipped the story on Andrea from yesterday's *Post*. He brought it out and let them read it before he went on to what his delving into the newspaper files had disclosed to him. "So you see," he said next, "there's not the least doubt it was Greg, is there?"

"But Miss Langdon always seemed so nice." Effie couldn't help grasping at straws. "If it was Greg she wouldn't have said she was alone at the fair. Why, it would be a terrible thing to do, not claim his body, let the poor little fellow be buried under a number and all. How could she do a thing like that?"

Seymour wasn't left to cope with such die-hard naïveté by himself. Walt cut in, "My God, Effie, be your age, will you? Miss Andrea Langdon—" he had the clipping in his hand and eyed Andrea's picture with a leer "—looks like butter wouldn't melt in her mouth, but it don't go down with me. She didn't claim the kid's body because then she'd have to admit he was hers and wouldn't that have made a great big juicy scandal, though." Walt smacked his lips to emphasize

103

how juicy it would have been and then turned thoughtful. "It hasn't lost any of its juice either. Not when you bring her father into it, a big shot like him running for Congress."

"I don't know —" Effie faltered. "I'm all mixed up about it. It was a terrible thing for her to do but when you stop to think about it — Greg was dead — there'd be disgrace for her and her father — what good would it do — but that note to thank me for the football helmet —" A withering glance from her husband put an end to her nervous outburst. She bent her head and began to pleat her apron.

Walt looked at Seymour. "What's your angle?" he demanded. "How was Greg related to you?"

"I was his father."

"That's the way I had it figured." Walt's smug tone made it clear that he always had things figured, that nobody could fool him.

"You were Greg's father?" Effie sat up straight. "Why didn't you marry Miss Langdon, a nice girl like her, and give your little boy a name? If you'd done what was right there'd have been none of this hole-in-a-corner business and poor little Greg," she began to cry again, "would be alive today, a son to be proud of —"

Seymour walked back and forth across the room and sat down again. "Believe me, Mrs. Horbal, I'll regret it all my life." His voice rang with conviction. Not even Walt could doubt that he meant what he said.

It didn't matter that his next words were wasted on the other man. They weren't meant for him but for Effie who had to have things prettied up, smoothed over. He said, "But you've got it all wrong, Mrs. Horbal. It was the other way around. Andrea wouldn't marry me." He went on to paint himself guiltless. Andrea had refused to marry him and gone away with friends. He'd tried to trace her, not daring, though, to approach her father. When he wrote to her she hadn't answered his letters. At last he'd stopped trying. His pride, after all, came into it. . . .

Then, after all these years, he'd found himself in Ridgeway and paid her a visit. She'd told him she'd had a miscarriage. He was ready to leave when Effie's gift arrived.

From this point on the truth would serve. He told about waiting outside, following Andrea, retrieving the football helmet from the pond, his realization that she had lied when she said her pregnancy ended in a miscarriage, his decision to stay on in Ridgeway and look up the Horbals in the hope that they could lead him to his son.

Effie was swayed, her sympathy for Andrea lessening a little. "She should have told you the truth about what happened to Greg. She should have told us the truth."

"And sent back the helmet," Walt inserted. "Cost four bucks, didn't it?"

"Oh, Walt, how can you joke when—"

"Who said I was joking? Four bucks is four

bucks." He sent a calculating glance to Seymour. "And it don't come so easy to me that I like to see it thrown in a pond. Of course Miss Langdon would never think of that. She don't know what it means to live on a workingman's pay."

"I should say not." Seymour met Walt's glance with sudden elation. They understood each other so perfectly that they were able to send wordless messages back and forth over Effie's not very bright head.

But it wasn't altogether a stupid head either, Seymour realized a moment later. After being lost in thought for an interval Effie said, "Greg was no unwanted child, Mr. Boyd. You could tell just from seeing Miss Langdon with him how much she loved him. I can't understand her not marrying you if it was like you say and you were ready to do the right thing by her."

"Well, she was very young at the time. I don't believe she really looked ahead to what her refusal would lead to."

"She always struck me as a girl who would look ahead," Effie said. "One who'd think things out."

"Effie, it's all water over the dam now," Walt said curtly. "It's none of your business anyway. It's between her and Mr. Boyd."

Effie subsided. But even though her tongue was silenced her mind was busy examining the story Seymour had told her, weighing it against her own knowledge of Andrea, and finding it

106

wanting; wondering why he had come to them with his troubles, when, as Walt said, it was all water over the dam now.

Seymour and he were talking about the fire. As she glanced at her husband, alarm stirred to life in her. He looked too pleased with himself. He was up to something. It was like when he'd made her sell aunt Elva's property in Nevada—she'd been a fool to give in to him about it but she never could stand up to him when he yelled at her—and now he looked the same way, like he'd looked when he talked so big about how he'd double her money in no time.

Effie's alarm mounted until it closed like an iron hand on her heart. Something was going on—

Walt said, "You go out and put a pot of coffee on the stove, Effie. You had your supper, Mr. Boyd?"

"No, I haven't, and to tell the truth," the charm was back in his smile but it was lost now on Effie, "I'm pretty hungry."

"Make him a couple of sandwiches while you're at it," Walt directed. "They'll hold him together until he can get a real meal."

Effie said nothing. She went on lagging feet to the kitchen.

A few minutes later her husband came out and closed the door between the kitchen and the dining room. The telephone was in the dining room. "I got to make a call," he said.

She measured water and coffee into the percolator, put it on the electric range, took bread from the pantry and cold meat from the refrigerator. Walt was on the telephone. She went to the dining-room door to listen.

He seemed to be talking to someone, identifying himself. Then, after a silence, he spoke again, his voice distinct and with a purring note in it. "How are you, Miss Langdon?" he said. "Yes, it's Walt Horbal. We had your note but Effie and me got to talking about Greg tonight and I thought I'd just call you up and ask if you wouldn't change your mind about giving us his address and letting us go to see him. We thought a lot of him, you know . . . Oh, I see . . . Yes, you said the same thing when you wrote . . . Well, I guess you have to do what you think is best . . . But will you at least remember us to him the next time you see him? . . . Okay, Miss Langdon. Good-by."

The click of the receiver told Effie he had hung up. She hurried back to the table and began to make sandwiches. Her hands shook so that the knife slipped and she cut her thumb. She had to run water on it to stop the bleeding. It was an omen, she thought. Whatever her husband was up to with the soft-spoken, lying Mr. Boyd, only trouble and the shedding of blood would come of it. If she tried to tell that to Walt, though, he would only laugh at her and say she was a superstitious fool. But she felt almost fey at the moment in her certainty that evil and blood would come of this visit from Seymour Boyd.

She arranged the sandwiches and coffee on a tray and carried it into the living room.

Seymour rose to take the tray from her and noticed the bandage on her thumb. "Oh, you've hurt yourself, Mrs. Horbal," he said.

"I cut my thumb." As she looked at him she wondered how he could ever have made a favorable impression on her the first time he came, and even for a while tonight. Well, he would never fool her again.

While he was eating with appreciative comment on how good the sandwiches were, Walt said, "Effie, I was telling Mr. Boyd we got some snapshots of Greg somewheres. You know where they are?"

"No, I don't." If she couldn't stop them in whatever they were plotting against poor Miss Langdon, at least she needn't help them, she thought.

But Walt didn't allow her to get away with it. He turned so ugly in his demands that she find their old album that at last she pretended she'd just remembered where it was and went upstairs and brought it down.

Tears blurred her eyes as she looked at the pictures of Greg. There weren't many. They had no camera themselves so there were just a few taken by an occasional visitor at the farm. Two of them were of Greg in his babyhood, another showed him at eighteen months, and the last two had been taken when he was two and a half.

"Hell," said Walt, looking in vain for later ones. "There must be some more. What about when your aunt Elva was here? She took a picture of us and I damn well remember she took at least one picture of Greg."

Effie looked at the pictures of Greg at two and a half, smiling in one, shy and solemn in the other, and wiped away tears. They didn't show him as he was just before his fifth birthday and, of course, he'd changed a lot by that time. She said in a choked voice, "He was just halfway through his poor little life when these pictures were taken."

She looked at Seymour as she said this and let her dislike show in her glance. It was his fault that Greg was dead. If he'd done the right thing and married Miss Langdon she wouldn't have had to hide Greg away; she wouldn't have been driving through Broome's Cove the day of the fire, and Greg would be alive today.

Walt said, "Snap out of it, Effie. You've carried on over the kid long enough. Try to remember what became of the pictures your aunt Elva took of him the last summer he was with us. She was here two weeks in July and died right after she went back to Nevada. Whatever pictures she took of Greg would show him just about the way he looked when he died. There couldn't have been much change in him in the little time he had left."

Effie winced at the callousness of it. The little boy had shared their roof, sat at their table for almost all of his short life. And yet Walt could speak like this. In the old days he'd pretended to be very fond of Greg, too.

She stared at her husband. Seymour was watching her and caught the flicker of hesitation on her face. Then she said, "I'm afraid they're gone, Walt, mixed up with a lot of old papers I threw out before we went to Nevada. I've never seen them since."

She was lying, Seymour told himself. Her moment of hesitation had given her away.

Walt hadn't noticed it. He swore loudly, declaring that she was the biggest fool of a woman a man ever got stuck with. She was supposed to be so neat, she couldn't have thrown the pictures out, he said. They must be around somewhere. They used to be in the secretary, didn't they?

He went over to the glass-fronted secretary and created chaos in the drawers and cubbyholes as he rummaged through them in a fruitless search for the pictures.

Effie bore his abusive language in silence. But her mouth was set, making a firm line in her thin face.

Let it go for the present, Seymour thought. He would have liked to approach Andrea with a snapshot of Greg in his hand but it didn't really matter, not for the preliminary touch, and perhaps not even when he was ready to approach her on the big one. . . .

He told Walt it was all right and not to worry about it. If they needed a picture of Greg one would turn up somewhere. Mrs. Horbal could probably find just the one they wanted.

"If she tries," he said. He smiled at Effie but his eyes were cold, warning her not to stand in his way.

"She goddamn well better," Walt growled, with a glare for his wife. "Of all the stupid women I ever met she takes the prize."

Effie maintained her silence. She kept her hands closed over each other to conceal the way they shook.

Seymour said good night. Walt walked to the door with him. Effie couldn't move. Her legs felt too weak to support her.

Chapter Nine

Andrea took Walt Horbal's call in the library. Across the hall were assembled the county political leaders her father had invited to dinner. She could hear them laughing over predinner drinks while she talked with Walt, trying to sound calm and matter of fact although her heart hammered against her ribs and her voice threatened to break every time she spoke.

It didn't cross her mind that he had found out Greg was four years dead; that refinement of cruelty in his inquiries escaped her. But she couldn't miss the spurious note in his pretense of friendliness or the menace that lay beneath it. She cut the call as short as she could and then sat on at the phone, incapable for the moment of returning to her father's guests and slipping back into her role of the young hostess displaying charming deference to a group of older men.

They saw her as a sheltered young woman who knew nothing of the darker side of life. They paid her elaborate compliments and told her father jokingly that he couldn't lose as long as he had her to show off in the campaign. He laughed and agreed, his pride in her a thing for all the world to see.

His pride in her, she thought numbly. How it could be humbled; how his campaign, with its stress on what an open record his personal, business, and civic careers had always been, could collapse around him if his daughter's past should come to light at this time.

And not only was there the question of his pride in her, she thought next; he loved her very much, too. In the past few years a new closeness had grown between them. When she was a little girl, lonely at times without a mother, she had loved her father but there hadn't been the closeness she felt toward him now. She hadn't known him well enough for it to develop. The demands of the expanding chain of Grocery Mart stores took him away from home much of the time. A little girl couldn't accompany him on business trips. A little girl going to school had to stay home under the supervision of her great-aunt Gertrude, elderly, severe, an inadequate substitute for a mother but the best her father could provide. Then, when her great-aunt died, there'd been boarding school, Miss Merrivale's, and Seymour, so much older than the boys she knew, his charm and warmth suddenly filling the loneliness of a lifetime. Then had come the New Year's Eve party, her first drinks to break down restraints . . . and Greg.

Greg. Andrea stared empty-eyed into the past.

If, in her desperation and disillusionment when Seymour vanished from her ken, she hadn't had kindhearted Mrs. Davenport, the house mother who had been so fond of her, to confide in; if Mrs. Davenport, now five years dead, retiring that spring after thirty years at Miss Merrivale's, hadn't been ready with a plan that took them to the remote Nebraska town where Greg was born; if her father hadn't been in Brazil that summer occupied with a project for buying a coffee plantation to supply his food chain; in short, if the way to concealment hadn't been possible for her, if she'd had to confide her plight in her father, he would have worked out a way to adopt Greg, who would not then have been in Broome's Cove to lose his life in the fire on that terrible day four years ago.

While he was in Oldfield she had thought she was doing her best for him and, in the meantime, building up her contact with the orphanage, pointing always toward the day when she would bring home Greg as a child awaiting placement and persuade her father to keep him. This was what she had planned to do the day of the fire. She had thought she was handling

115

the whole thing so well; that her chief concerns were to protect her father from the grief of knowing the truth about Greg and to safeguard Greg himself, with his Nebraska birth certificate that had him born in wedlock, from the stigma of illegitimacy.

But of course that hadn't been it at all, Andrea acknowledged wearily to herself. She had been safeguarding her own reputation. She had thought she loved her son wholeheartedly but she had turned him over to the Horbals when he was four months old—taking great pains with her false name, rented car, and post-office box number to keep her true identity from them—and thereafter salved her conscience with visits and presents and her plan for introducing him into her own home; but only when she felt there would be no questions raised, no risks involved for her.

Greg had paid with his life for her not having loved him enough, for not putting his interests ahead of her own.

This was the cross she bore and would have to bear for the rest of her days. It had made her an outsider, standing always a little apart from life, cut off from the normal pattern of marriage by her feeling that she would have to tell her prospective husband about Greg.

This was beyond her, a thing sealed off so completely that she had become incapable of telling anyone about it.

116

And now the Horbals meant to blackmail her over it. There was no evading the prospect; it had to be faced. Blackmail was to be added to her punishment for her sins of omission and commission for which Greg had paid with his blameless young life.

This thought was no more than an extension of her usual forms of self-flagellation. It was designed to stiffen her courage for what lay ahead of her but it failed of its purpose. Unbidden, the thought of Fergus came into her mind. What if the Horbals took money from her (the good home she'd found for Greg had been with potential blackmailers) and then talked anyway? What if the story came out in the open and Fergus heard about it?

"Andrea." Her father stood in the doorway. "It's time we—is anything wrong?" He had caught a glimpse of her stricken face before she could manage a smile for him.

"No, Father. I'm a little tired, that's all, and taking a respite from political labors." She went to him and slipped her arm through his. "Shall we feed your cohorts, Congressman?"

He laughed and told her not to count her chickens before they were hatched.

They went back across the hall. Andrea resumed her role of charming young hostess. This, too, was part of her cross.

* * *

117

The next afternoon Seymour paid his fellow worker another five dollars for the use of the jalopy again. He didn't phone Andrea that he was about to visit her. He felt confident that after last night's call from Walt Horbal she would be home, afraid to leave, wondering from what direction the next blow would fall and what form it would take.

He went to his hotel from the lunchroom, changed his clothes, and set out for Andrea's, telling himself on the way that this was his last ride in the jalopy. Tomorrow he'd buy himself a secondhand car of later vintage and in far better condition than this piece of junk. Clothes, too, including a topcoat now that the weather had turned chilly. He would move into the Wilton, the best hotel in Ridgeway, and a world above the fleabag he now called home. Tomorrow night he'd pick out a good restaurant, have a first-class meal, maybe find himself a woman, and for just the one evening let down his self-imposed restrictions on drinking. Not to really let himself go, of course, at this stage of the game, but just enough to feel good and relax a little. There was, after all, a certain amount of strain involved in what he was doing and he needed a few hours off from it. By God, he told himself, slowing down to turn off the road at Hopewell Farm, when this thing was over and he shook himself loose from Ridgeway he'd buy a case of Old Grand Dad, hole up somewhere, and stay drunk until it was gone. That was just what he'd need after what he was putting up with now, getting up in the middle of the night to work eight solid hours in a dive like Frankie's Handy Lunchroom, scraping filthy plates, washing filthy dishes, limiting his drinks at a time when his whole system clamored for them under the strain of figuring all the angles of his project—call it Operation Blackmail—getting pally with trash like the Horbals, worrying and stewing over having the prize, so near, so glittering, somehow snatched away at the last minute—when he thought of all he was going through, he'd have earned the right to hole up and stay drunk for a month when it was over.

That was just what he'd do. Christ, if he could only do it now! There'd never been a time when he'd had so great a need for the easement of alcohol, the welcome oblivion it would bring.

He stopped the jalopy at the front door of the Hopewell Farm, got out, cast a bitter glance over the house and grounds—but why nag himself with what might-have-been?—went up the front steps and rang the bell.

Andrea, summoned by the maid, came downstairs. Her face was expressionless. But of course she'd been forewarned; he'd had to give his name to the maid.

Under her pale brown fringe of hair her eyes rested on him remotely as if not quite seeing him, as if he didn't quite exist. Unexpectedly, a

119

mixture of feelings came to life in him for a moment. Once upon a time this lovely statue hadn't looked at him like this. Once upon a time—

He looked at her again. She wore heather wool and handsewn brogues. Everything about her spelled money, he reflected, hating her violently for the pampered daughter of wealth that she was, a stranger to hunger, the lack of a roof over her head, the cruelty of a family that disowned her; hating her so much for having all and far more than he had forfeited years ago that he made a last-minute change of approach. Instead of going straight to the point he decided to make it a game of cat-and-mouse to prolong the agony for her.

"Shall we go in the library?" her tone was as remote as her expression.

He declined a seat when she sat down. "I'll stand," he said. "I feel a bit restless, a bit out of sorts. Are you surprised to see me here when you thought I'd gone to Washington?"

She examined the question. "No, not really," she said, her glance a little less remote as she assessed his appearance. He looked better than the last time, she thought, his face not quite such a gaunt ruin. (She didn't know, of course, about the regular meals and hours, the rationed drinks during Operation Blackmail.) He wore better clothes, too. He might have been almost anyone dropping in to see her.

He strolled to a window and back. "I couldn't make up my mind to leave," he said softly. "I have no ties, you know, and I'm getting older. I've been thinking about you a lot, Andrea; what we might have had together, that sort of thing."

She made no reply. He wandered around the room and stopped at the liquor cabinet. "Shall I make you a drink?" he inquired, pouring himself a bourbon and emptying the glass in one swallow.

"No."

Damn her to hell for sitting there looking at him as if he were something that came from outer space. Let her have it right now.

"I've been more or less floating around in this vicinity," he said, eying her narrowly. "And a little farther away in eastern Connecticut. To be exact, I've been visiting some old acquaintances of yours in Oldfield."

She had thought she was prepared for almost anything. But this was a blow beyond the limits of her imagination. Beyond speech, her face drained of color, she looked at him.

"Don't you think you were very unfair to me when you said you had a miscarriage?" he reproached her. "Haven't I the right to know I have a son?" He was careful to employ the present tense. He would reveal no knowledge yet of the grave in Broome's Cove cemetery.

"No." She could barely speak. "You have—no

121

rights whatsoever." Her voice strengthened a little. "You lost them ten years ago."

He looked sorrowful. "I know how I treated you and I've regretted it ever since. But can't we let bygones be bygones, Andrea? Can't I have at least one meeting with my son?"

It seemed her face could turn no whiter; but at this request it did. "No," she said. "No . . ."

"Oh, he's too good for me?" He frowned, but a faint grin broke through his mask of sorrow. Why hadn't she noticed ten years ago that he had a fox's face with a cruel, sly fox's grin?

She stood up. "Will you go now, please? And don't come back. Ever."

He didn't move. One hand jingled change in his pocket. He took out a coin, tossed it into the air, and caught it. "Shall I take up the question of my rights with your father? He knows, of course, that he has a grandson?" When no reply came from her he added, "By the time I bought a few clothes and things out of the hundred you gave me before, I didn't have enough to leave on. I had to find a job in Ridgeway. But it pays very little. So I'm more or less stuck here."

She studied him, the man who had her at his mercy. "How much do you feel you'd have to have to leave now?"

Seymour had his figure set. It was modest, designed merely to soften her up for the big one. "Fifteen hundred would do it," he said.

"Five hundred for the Horbals, a thousand for me. Just a small stake to give me a fresh start somewhere." He paused. "Don't think it's easy for me to do this to you, Andrea. When I think of the family I came from," his drawl thickened to honey softness, "and the raising I had, I don't feel very pleased with myself. But I'm desperate for a fresh start, Andrea. I have no choice but to—"

"Blackmail me?"

He looked hurt. "Must you put it that way?"

"There is no other way to put it. And if I give you this money you will leave the state?"

"Yes. And not come near you again."

She didn't believe him but whether she did or not was beside the point for the present. She had to get rid of him now, buy a breathing space. He wouldn't dare to come back for several weeks, at least not until the election was over, she thought, underestimating his greed and capacity for cruelty, judging him a little, in spite of herself, by normal standards. If he came back, then she would have to do something, she didn't know what, to rid herself of him and the Horbals, people to whom she had entrusted her son and who turned out to be blackmailers like her son's father.

"Very well," she said. "I'll get the money tomorrow."

"Shall I come here to collect it?"

"No. Where are you staying?"

"The Lincoln. You never heard of it, I'm sure." He spoke with irony. "But there's a restaurant, Smalley's Grill, over two blocks on the corner of Smalley and Main. It's quite respectable. You can meet me there at ten tomorrow morning with the money. And smallish bills, please, nothing larger than twenties. Unmarked bills, of course." His fox's grin carried a warning. "If I got picked up with marked bills, how I would talk!"

"There'll be no marked bills. Will you leave, please?"

The doorbell rang as he turned to go. The maid answered it, admitted Fergus MacDonald, and held the door open for Seymour. He moved toward it at a deliberate pace, eying Fergus coolly, being eyed coolly in return, saying "Excuse me" as he brushed past him, giving no ground.

Fergus turned and looked after him. He'd never seen him before. The old heap parked outside must belong to him. Fergus had noticed it because it wasn't the type of car he expected to see in Andrew Langdon's driveway. But for all his soft voice, head held high, and arrogant stare, the man going out the door fitted in with the car, Fergus thought. He had a dissipated look and around him hung an aura of failure.

What was he doing at Langdon's?

The maid took Fergus to the library. He didn't stay long. The moment he saw Andrea he knew she was under a great strain, for all her effort to behave as if nothing was the matter. He accepted a drink and she had one with him. She needed it, he thought. It brought a little color back to her face and helped her to relax.

He had intended to ask her for a date but this wasn't the time to do it. He said he'd see her tomorrow night at the dinner for her father and left, asking himself on the way out to his car, "Now what was that all about? What did that guy say to Andrea to get her so upset?"

He thought about it as he drove back to Ridgeway to his office. He wasn't jealous of the other man, the unexplained stranger—at least he didn't think he was—but he couldn't understand the effect his visit had had on Andrea. She hadn't mentioned the man. There was no reason why she should, of course. She didn't have to account to Fergus for other visitors at the house. Visitors? The word implied a friendly relationship, however casual. In that sense the man had been no visitor. He had left Andrea on the edge of going to pieces.

When Fergus reached his office, before he went to his desk he stopped at the library to check on state-wide election figures he needed in a piece he was writing for tomorrow's paper.

As always, the youthful attendant was ready for a chat with Fergus, who was a favorite of his.

"Say," he said, as Fergus leaned on the

counter and lit a cigarette, "I forgot to tell you we had another guy in a couple of days ago reading up on Little Sir 915 and the Broome's Cove fire."

"Anyone I know?" Fergus spoke with no particular interest, but he knew most of the newspapermen in the state who might be doing a feature story on the little boy.

"Well, maybe you do, but he was nobody I ever saw before. Tall guy, kind of a thin face, red hair, soft voice."

"Oh." Fergus eyed the young attendant with dawning interest. All the way from Andrea's he had been thinking about a tall, thin-faced man with red hair and a voice that was soft as it said "Excuse me."

There must be lots of men who answered that description, Fergus reminded himself. Then he asked, "How old a guy would you say?"

The attendant hesitated. "It's a little hard to say. He looked like someone who'd been around—"

Dissipated face, Fergus thought, his interest growing.

"Maybe he was thirty-seven or eight. Not a whole lot older than that."

There was little point in asking how he was dressed—men changed their suits—but Fergus asked anyway.

"Gray suit," the attendant said.

The man leaving Andrea's had been wearing a gray suit.

"He tell you what paper or magazine he was with?"

"Nope. Sort of ducked around it. And when we were talking about why the kid was never identified he wouldn't even say what his theory on it was. I told him mine. You know, about the foreigners who were—"

"I know," Fergus cut in, having heard the theory many times.

"So then he said something kind of funny. He said he might give a talk on his theory to a select audience of one person." The attendant paused. "Wasn't that a cockeyed thing for him to say, though?"

"Yes it was," Fergus said but he didn't mean it. Yesterday Andrea had run away from the very mention of the fire, which was, after all, four years behind her. Today she'd been very much upset by a visit from the man who'd looked up the fire in the *Post* files a couple of days ago. At least it seemed reasonable to assume it was the same man, Fergus thought. The questionable point was whether or not Andrea was the select audience of one for whom his talk on the unidentified little boy was intended. Fergus could see no possible connection between the little boy and her.

Andrea, at this time, sat at her desk looking at the balance of $1548.25 in her checkbook. It would be very low after she cashed a check for Seymour tomorrow. She had no money of her own coming in until the first of the month and would have to go to her father for an advance on her allowance. He would shake his head indulgently and ask her how in the world she managed to get rid of money so fast.

Seymour returned the jalopy to its owner and told the proprietor of Frankie's that he'd have to take tomorrow off. The proprietor didn't like it but had long since become resigned to the vagaries of kitchen help.

Seymour went from the lunchroom to a used-car lot nearby. He selected a clean-looking 1953 Chevrolet on sale for four hundred dollars and paid twenty dollars down on it. He had almost no money left but it didn't matter. He would have fifteen hundred tomorrow.

He made arrangements with the salesman to pay the balance due and have the car registered and ready to turn over to him by ten o'clock the next morning.

He felt satisfied with the day's accomplishments as he went on to a restaurant for dinner.

Later in the evening, though, nursing along his third drink in a bar, he was not so satisfied. His thoughts had turned to Effie Horbal.

Chapter Ten

At ten o'clock the next morning in Smalley's Grill, Andrea gave Seymour a Manila envelope containing fifteen hundred dollars in twenty-dollar bills.

He said, "Thanks, Andrea, and good-by. I'll be out of Ridgeway in another hour or two."

She didn't answer. Without having spoken at all, she turned and left the restaurant.

By ten-thirty Seymour was in possession of the car on which he had made a down payment yesterday. By eleven o'clock he had checked out of his former hotel into the Wilton where he took a room with a private bath, this last a luxury his previous lodging and none before it for a long time had offered.

The Wilton also offered a men's bar. He stopped in and had two bourbons. But he was conscious of the time and by eleven-thirty he was on his way to Oldfield at the wheel of his own car. It was Effie he wanted to see. With Walt at work he hoped to find her home alone in the middle of the day.

Last night he had given her a lot of thought. She was the weak spot in his project, not because she could infect her husband with her doubts and scruples but through her own knowledge of what was going on. If anything went wrong, if any unforeseen factor arose, there was no telling what Effie would do. That was why he was on his way to see her. If he had a chance to talk with her in Walt's absence he could draw her out, weigh her attitude, and then be in a better position to decide just how much of a potential threat she represented.

At the very least, she was a nuisance. For one thing, there was the picture of the kid Walt had mentioned. She had lied the other night when she said she'd thrown it out with some old papers. She knew where it was; she had it put away somewhere. Seymour hadn't made an issue of it at the time but today it would be a different story. If she thought for one minute that he was going to put up with that sort of thing from her she was damn well mistaken. . . .

Mile after mile he thought about Effie. His good mood of the morning soured and then turned vicious over the trouble she was causing him. What was she, anyway? A moronic little mouse, a piece of trash scared of her own shadow. He'd put the fear of God into her today. He'd make her understand that she counted for nothing, less than nothing, where he was concerned. Christ, when he stopped to think about it; she had her nerve holding out on him and her husband the other night about the kid's picture. Scurrying around, shaking like a leaf, but lying to them, holding out —

He'd fix her, though. He'd show her today where she stood.

He stopped at a wayside bar outside of Oldfield for two more bourbons. They did not improve his mood. By the time he reached the house he had worked himself into a state that was all the more dangerous for being concealed beneath a show of politeness toward Effie when she came to the door.

She looked taken aback at the sight of him. "Walt's not home," she said. "He's at work."

"Yes, I know. I'm calling on you, Mrs. Horbal. May I come in?" His foot was already over the threshold, allowing her no choice in the matter.

She took him into the sitting room and perched on a chair in the same apprehensive manner as on his last visit. "What did you want to see me about, Mr. Boyd? I was just going to start my ironing."

"I won't keep you long." He still smiled. "I thought I'd pick up the picture your aunt took of Greg a few weeks before he died."

Her mouth opened. "But I told Walt—"

"I know what you told Walt." Seymour's smile faded. "However, it was perfectly plain to me that you were lying. Don't imagine for one moment, Mrs. Horbal, that the picture is of much importance in the project your husband and I are working on. What is important is your unco-operative attitude. I don't like it, Mrs. Horbal. I don't intend to put up with it. Suppose you show me that you're prepared to change it by giving me the picture without further discussion or delay."

Anger fired Effie's meek spirit. "I don't like your attitude either, Mr. Boyd," she declared. "You've got no right to come into my house and talk to me like this. And whatever you're planning about Miss Langdon, I don't care to be mixed up in it in any way whatsoever."

"Before we go into that, where is the picture, Mrs. Horbal?" Seymour's slight control of himself vanished completely. Obstinacy was a trait he had never been able to tolerate in others. But Effie missed the deadly quality of the glance he gave her; her own glance had gone involuntarily to the row of books in the secretary.

"Oh, so that's where it is." He moved swiftly to the secretary and opened the glass-paned doors. "Hidden in one of the books, Mrs. Horbal?"

She sprang to her feet. "You leave those books alone and get out of here this very minute!"

He took the books out one by one and shook them, thrusting her aside with a sweep of his arm when she tried to stop him.

"Leave them alone!" Effie rushed at him again, lost to caution, more tiger than mouse in her anger.

A picture dropped out of one of the books. He caught it in mid-air and looked at it. It was the picture of a smiling little boy in shorts and jersey, squinting a little in the summer sunlight. It was a picture to wring the heart of anyone who knew that a few weeks after it was taken the little boy would be dead. But the little boy's father gave no thought to this. He glanced at the picture just long enough to assure himself it was the proof of identity he sought and started to put it in his pocket.

Effie grabbed at it and tore it in two, getting hold of half of it herself. She tore her half into smaller pieces before he knocked her down and snatched at them.

"You stupid little devil, look what you've done," he shouted at her.

Effie was back on her feet, beside herself in an outburst of fury that equaled his. "Get out of my house!" she screamed. "And don't ever come back or I'll call the police; I'll tell them what you're up to; I'll tell them—"

She saw his eyes then and stopped short, her voice cut off by terror for her life that came too late. She turned and ran screaming for help, Seymour after her, blocking her off from the hall. She ran through the dining room, instinct directing her flight toward the back door and out of the confinement of the house where no one could hear her screams. She had no time to think that outside there was no one to hear her either, no help to come from any source. All she could do was run.

She got as far as the kitchen. The cellar went down from it. She had been in the cellar a few minutes before Seymour arrived and the door stood open. He caught her as she was running past it.

She had no chance at all. If she had been pitting her strength against his under normal conditions, she would have had little chance of getting away from him; in his white-hot fury she had none. He caught her around the waist, swung her high in the air, and threw her with brutal force headfirst down the cellar stairs.

One more scream came from her. Then she hit the cement floor with sickening force and lay crumpled and still, with blood pouring out of her head. The terrible moment of murder, the moment of accomplishment during which murderer and victim were fused into one, was over. She was dead.

Seymour's fury ran out of him like air out of a pricked balloon. For a timeless interval he looked down at her. He had killed her. He had committed murder. Through the long misspent years he had been moving always toward this house, these stairs, this woman dead on the cellar floor.

But he felt nothing. He stood apart from what he had done as if it were the work of other hands.

A clock ticked behind him in the kitchen. That was the only sound at first. Then his ears picked up the drip of a faucet out of time with the clock.

Presently a sense of urgency began to fill the vacuum within him. The ticking clock was a reminder that time did not stand still, that by remaining here he courted the danger of Walt coming home early from work or someone else arriving or a car passing the house and the driver noticing his car in the yard. He had to break the compelling tie that bound him to the dead woman and go.

But first he had to take a closer look at her. He went down the cellar stairs and bent over

135

her body. Her eyes were open and seemed to look up at him. But they were vacant and beginning to glaze. The pool of blood around her head was beginning to congeal.

Only a little while ago she was alive. How could it all have blown up so suddenly, the scuffle over the picture, the blow he gave her, her threat to call the police, her flight, her small, slight body hurtling down the stairs to die? He hadn't meant it to happen so . . . Or had he? Through the long misspent years. . . .

He gave himself a shake and turned away. By the time he was back upstairs the curious interlude was over. His mind started to function again. He had to think of his own preservation.

He had touched nothing in the kitchen or dining room. He went on to the sitting room, picked up the scattered books, wiped them with his handkerchief, and replaced them on the shelf. He closed the glass-paned doors and wiped the knobs. A small rug was scuffed up near the dining-room door. He straightened it out. That was all there was to do.

He left by the front door. There was no one in sight. He opened and closed the door with his handkerchief wrapped around his hand.

But he was a long way yet from being safe. Prospects of disaster shook him as he got into his car and backed out of the yard. Suppose he had engine trouble or a flat tire to hold him up on this road? Suppose he was seen by children playing somewhere on it? Suppose another car came along?

He wiped sweat off his face with his sleeve and drove very carefully to avoid the least chance of a mishap. The gravel road unfolded before him with agonizing slowness. God, would he ever get off it?

No children played on it. The deserted farmhouse presented blank shuttered windows to his anxious gaze as he went past. No car came toward him.

He reached the blacktop road at last and turned left toward Oldfield. He began to breathe a little easier. Not much, but a little. If a car should pass him now, it would look as if he were coming from Hotchkissville.

None did. He had almost reached the center of Oldfield before he encountered his first car, a truck whose driver didn't even glance his way.

He went on through the town. As he passed the general store in a sudden burst of speed he didn't dare turn his head to see if the storekeeper's wife was at her usual post in the window. He had to hope that she wasn't.

Oldfield was soon left behind. His foot went down harder on the accelerator. In another minute he was traveling at fifty, the posted speed limit, with every turn of the wheels increasing his sense of safety.

A few miles farther on, the road joined the highway that would take him back to Ridgeway. Now he was really safe, he thought. He might have been anywhere in his car; there was nothing in the world to connect him with the dead woman in the cellar in Oldfield.

As long as there wasn't, he was prepared to admit to himself that her death served a certain purpose after all. It removed the weak spot in his project. Walt Horbal, God knew, was out for all he could get and would go along with anything Seymour proposed.

He thought about Walt and what his position would be in connection with his wife's death. Unless he took it into his head to come home from work early today he would be safe too. . . .

Walt didn't leave work that day until closing time at the mill. Then he stopped in a Hotchkissville tavern and had two beers with a fellow worker. It was five o'clock and Effie had been dead for three hours before Walt reached home, called her name, saw the open cellar door, and found her.

Their family doctor was also the medical examiner. He summoned the resident state policeman who represented law and order in Oldfield.

No suspicion rested on Walt after the state policeman verified his statement that he had

138

been at work at the estimated time of death. With no signs of a struggle, nothing to indicate that Effie hadn't been alone in the house when she died, an accidental fall would be given as the cause of death on the death certificate.

Chapter Eleven

The twenty-five-dollar-a-plate dinner being given for Andrew Langdon by the Ridgeway County Republican Women's Club was scheduled for seven o'clock that evening in the Wilton ballroom. Fergus arrived at the hotel at six-thirty, found three of his colleagues in the bar and refreshed himself in their company until it was time to go up to the ballroom.

It was seven o'clock then but the dinner wasn't going to start on schedule. The head table was unoccupied and although many people were seated at the tables for eight, almost as many more were still milling about, not ready to settle down yet. The walls were hung with pictures of Republican notables, Andrew Langdon's, in back of the head table, the largest one of all. Posters filled in the blank spaces, exhorting the voter to win with Langdon, give Ike a Republican Congress, get out the vote, vote the straight Republican ticket. It was too bad, Fergus reflected as he glanced around the room, that pictures and posters weren't reversible with Democratic faces and slogans on the other side of them. It would make things simpler for the committee in charge of tomorrow night's Democratic dinner.

He took his seat at the press table. Earlier arrivals had already counted the gate. So far, he was informed, two hundred and ten paying guests had arrived. His colleagues were impressed. "After all," one remarked, "Langdon's not running for the presidency. It's only a seat in the House."

"Well, he's loaded with dough himself," another said. "He's got a lot of rich friends turning out to support him. They got to look after their own. If they don't, who will?"

"He could kick in the whole cost of his campaign himself and never notice it," someone else said. "Only, hell, it wouldn't look right to Republican ditchdiggers."

The speaker was challenged to name a Republican ditchdigger and was inventing ribald names when Chuck Grennan bustled over with hearty greetings and mimeographed copies of the candidate's speech.

Last-minute arrivals were still coming in. The

estimate of the take was revised upward at the press table. Expenses were guessed at.

"God knows, the ladies' liquor bill will be nil," someone complained. "I remember one dinner two years ago with bottles of scotch and rye on every table."

"That one was a hundred a plate," Fergus said. "Who ever heard of free drinks at a mere twenty-five?"

It was ten minutes past seven. Enthusiastic applause burst out as Andrew Langdon came into the room through a door near the head table. He smiled and bowed in acknowledgement. Fergus's glance instantly sought Andrea in the group accompanying him. She was wearing a pale pink dinner dress. Her face was faintly flushed. She smiled her lovely smile and looked serene and beautiful.

There were twelve people settling themselves at the head table. The mayor of Ridgeway, being a Democrat, was not, of course, among the honored guests; instead, there was the mayor of a nearby Republican stronghold; there were the state chairman, the incumbent state senator from that district, the candidate for county sheriff, the county chairman, Chuck Grennan; there was an overstuffed lady Fergus didn't recognize; an understuffed lady he identified as president of the Ridgeway County Republican Women's Club; a lady of middle size who was

142

vice-chairman of the county committee and had the formidable look of one born to preside at party caucuses; there were two clergymen.

"Tonight we've got a rabbi and a priest," someone at the press table noted. "Too bad they can't figure out a way to work in a prayer in the middle of the dinner so they wouldn't have to wait until next time to invite a minister."

"They could call it an 'invodiction'," someone else suggested.

The overstuffed lady identified herself as chairman of the dinner with a short speech of welcome and added, "Will you please remain standing after our national anthem while Rabbi Goldberg gives the invocation?"

Everyone rose. From a record player somewhere out of sight the strains of THE STAR SPANGLED BANNER filled the room, catching a hapless waiter bending over a table with a tray of relishes. He straightened to what was more or less attention and almost dropped the heavy tray.

When the anthem came to an end, the rabbi invoked God's blessing on the gathering and what they were about to eat and accomplish. Everyone sat down. Fresh shrimp in bowls of cracked ice were already at each place. The meal began.

Fergus faced the head table. By the time

143

breast of pheasant was served, Andrea had picked him out of the gathering and given him a private smile. Seated beside her, Chuck Grennan, not too subtly, was counting the house.

Dessert was ice cream, molded into an imposing replica of the national Capitol. Wheeled in on a cart to the accompaniment of the TORE-ADOR SONG, it brought cheers and applause. Then there were only coffee and speeches left.

The overstuffed lady rose, rattling a spoon against a glass to command attention. She adjusted the microphone and announced that she had the honor of presenting Mrs. Alfred Hunt Thorndyke, president of the Ridgeway County Republican Women's Club, whose leadership and untiring industry in their common cause offered an inspiration to all who had the privilege of knowing and working with her.

Mrs. Thorndyke, the understuffed lady, rose, thanked the chairman of the dinner, thanked the paying guests for their generous response to this fund-raising project on behalf of their splendid candidate whom they all felt they wanted to work for just as hard as they could. Then, after a slight contretemps over misplaced eyeglasses, she read telegrams of good wishes from state Republicans in and out of high office, including one from the retiring congressman from the Sixth District, who was too ill to be present.

From that point on, Mrs. Thorndyke became a person much privileged. It became her privilege to introduce the state chairman; the mayor of the adjacent city, a good gray party wheel horse; the state senator and the candidate for county sheriff; the county chairman and vice-chairman. Andrea evoked a maternal note. Rabbi Goldberg of Emanuel Synagogue they had already had the pleasure of hearing in his fine invocation; Father Mullen, pastor of St. Michael's, would later give the benediction.

Mrs. Thorndyke's list of lesser privileges was now complete. A pause marked a hurried search of her notes. "And now," she said, finding her place, "I'm not going to take up your time with a long introduction of the distinguished gentleman who is our guest of honor tonight. Whatever I might say in praise of him, his successful business career, his wholehearted public service to our city and its environs, his eminent fitness for the highest office it is presently within our capacity to bestow upon him—"

Chuck Grennan nodded and beamed confidently as if to say that not only the governorship but the presidency was within the candidate's reach.

"—would be gilding the lily." Mrs. Thorndyke smiled prettily on the gathering.

"Why can't people get that quotation right?"

145

a colleague muttered in Fergus's ear.

"And so, ladies and gentlemen, it becomes my very great privilege to introduce to you our next congressman from the Sixth District, Mr. Andrew Langdon . . . Mr. Langdon."

There were cheers and applause as Langdon rose. He thanked Mrs. Thorndyke and stood smiling and relaxed until the hubbub subsided.

"Fellow citizens," he began and then, after a pause, "I can't say fellow Republicans since I have noticed several people here who aren't registered Republicans and yet have done me the kindness of attending this dinner. I should like particularly to thank them and, indeed, to thank all of you . . ."

He was launched. His speech, touching on state and national issues, wasn't bad as political speeches went, Fergus thought. He offered no hard and fast formulas for solving the grave problems of the times. He spoke simply and directly of all that he had to learn if he was elected and the effort he would make to learn it. He criticized the program of his Democratic opponent with good-tempered restraint. In general, he talked well and intelligently.

"He's learning fast," one of the gentlemen of the press observed. "He fumbled a bit a few weeks ago. Now he can sell himself — all he's got to sell so far — with one hand tied behind his back."

"Chuck Grennan's a smart cooky. He's got in his licks," another said.

Fergus reminded them that Andrew Langdon, in himself, had plenty to sell without help from Chuck Grennan, and realized with amusement that he went to the older man's defense mainly because he was Andrea's father.

The speech came to an end. The warm applause given to it was a tribute to the man more than to what he had said.

The overstuffed lady stood up, thanked Langdon, and told him that he had inspired them all to go out and work harder than ever for victory on November 4. Father Mullen, she then said, would pronounce the benediction.

Afterward Fergus assessed the crowd surging forward to shake hands with the candidate. It was made up, of course, of true believers; even a novice at politics would recognize that. But still . . . Langdon had the spark, the spontaneity, the natural liking for people of a born politician. The outline for tomorrow's piece took shape in Fergus's mind as he watched the scene: How much of a factor Langdon the man, the outgoing personality, would turn out to be in stemming the Democratic tide now spreading out into the safe Republican Sixth District.

Andrea was lost to sight among the well-wishers surrounding her father. Fergus held back, waiting for the group to thin out before he went up to speak to her.

Seymour Boyd came into the ballroom, halting just inside the archway to look around him. If he noticed Fergus he gave no sign of recognition. The latter looked at him. Not the gray suit tonight. (Seymour had taken his mind off murder in the early afternoon by going shopping after he got back to Ridgeway.) He presented an appearance of casual elegance in well-cut slacks and jacket, gray shirt and deeper gray tie. But as he moved toward the head table, Fergus saw that he was very drunk, walking with extreme care like someone balancing himself on the edge of a precipice and making elaborate bows and apologies to people who blocked his path.

Fergus started after him.

Andrea, momentarily on the outskirts of the group around her father, saw Seymour coming toward her. She had tried to believe he was hours gone from Ridgeway; but here he was, and drunk, too. Her trapped look was like a cry for help to Fergus, drawing him to the head table as fast as he could go in the crowded room.

But by the time he reached Andrea, she'd had no choice but to introduce Seymour to her father.

There were others present who'd had drinks

before the dinner. But there was no one else who exuded such an overpowering odor of liquor or whose gait was so unsteady or speech so slurred. Andrew Langdon raised his eyebrows involuntarily and shot a questioning glance at his daughter, while Seymour pumped his hand with unnecessary vigor and exclaimed, "Won'rful speech, Congressman. Won'rful. Gave 'em hell, 'swhat you did. Keep it up, give 'em hell, 'at's the way to do it. Goddamn fools, whole pack of them, 'at's what they are. Yessir, goddamn fools . . ."

He rambled on offensively. The older man freed his hand and turned away from him.

Seymour braced himself against the table. "Now look here, sir, you wan' my vote, don' you start highhattin' me or I'll—"

"Seymour, please!" Andrea's face flamed with embarrassment. People were beginning to stare.

Fergus came up. His arrival created a diversion. Seymour looked at him with drunken puzzlement, trying to remember where he'd seen him before.

Andrea said in a stifled voice, "Mr. Boyd . . . Mr. MacDonald," and Fergus shook hands with Seymour although it went against his grain to do it.

They were being edged away from Andrew Langdon by new arrivals. Seymour, haughtily telling a man who brushed against him to

149

watch out where he was going and with lordly air waving aside a proffered apology, forgot that Langdon had rebuffed him. He said, "Dryer'n hell around here. I'm going back down to the bar. Join me for a drink, Andrea?"

"No, thank you."

He looked her up and down with bleary-eyed insolence. "Then if you'll excuse me, I'll leave now. But I'll be seein' you, Andrea." He bowed so deeply that he almost fell and only saved himself by clutching Fergus's arm for support. A moment later he was gone, weaving his way out of the room with the same extreme care that had marked his entrance.

When he was out of sight, Andrea looked at Fergus with haunted eyes and said, "I'm not feeling very well, Fergus. Would you be so kind as to take me home? I'll tell Father I'm leaving and meet you by the cloakroom."

During the drive to Hopewell Farm she was past pretense, past trying to find a plausible explanation for the scene Fergus had witnessed. Huddled in silent misery, she had nothing at all to say.

Fergus was silent, too, knowing that was what she wanted. But when he stopped in front of the house and got out of the car to open her door for her he said, "Andrea, will you let me help you? I know you need help."

"Thank you, but there's nothing—" She

stepped out of the car and stood for a moment looking around her and up at the velvety night sky but not at him.

He tried again. "Andrea—"

"Its no use. It's a—well, it's a thing I have to handle alone." Her voice was a wisp of sound, so forlorn and hopeless that he ached to comfort her.

"But there must be something I can do," he said.

"No." She shook her head quickly. "No. There's nothing you can do except to forget everything that's happened tonight."

Before he could reply she fled up the steps and rang the bell. As he started after her a maid opened the door and Andrea said over her shoulder, "Good night, Fergus. Thank you for bringing me home."

The door closed after her. He stood looking at it and had no trouble picturing what was going on inside the house. Andrea would speak to the maid, trying to sound as if nothing were wrong. In another moment she would escape to her room and, with the door closed on the world, she would burst into tears.

He felt like forcing his way in to comfort her. But that was out of the question.

He drove back to the Wilton. Boyd had said he was going downstairs to the bar. It was quite possible that he was still there and that a conversation with him while his tongue was loosened by alcohol might bear some result.

Fergus meant to help Andrea in spite of herself.

But Seymour, although still in the bar, was past conversation, turning a blank, glassy stare on Fergus when he arrived. Soon thereafter, one of the bartenders summoned a bellboy who steered him to the elevator and took him up to his room, with Fergus trailing after them into the lobby.

He knew most of the personnel in the better hotels of Ridgeway and at the desk had no trouble finding out Seymour's full name and that he had registered only this morning, giving Durham, North Carolina, as his address.

This morning. But yesterday he had been at Andrea's and two days before that at the *Post* looking up the Broome's Cove fire. When had he arrived in town? Pondering the matter, Fergus thought he had probably been around for a couple of weeks, that it was his arrival that had brought about the change in Andrea. Where had he been staying until today, though?

It was ten o'clock. The lobby was quiet, the desk clerk not busy. Fergus asked for the night security officer with whom he had long maintained a friendly acquaintance.

The night security officer, whose name was Condon, was summoned from some other part of the hotel. He took Fergus into his office and, when he heard what he wanted, went off to confer with the bellboy who had steered Seymour up to his room. Presently he came back to report on what he had found out. Seymour, he said, had had only one small suitcase with him when he registered this morning, but just before six o'clock tonight the bellboy had carried several boxes from Schaefer's up to his room.

Schaefer's was the best men's store in Ridgeway. Fergus immediately connected it with the sartorial splendor Seymour was currently displaying.

The bellboy had also mentioned a bottle of bourbon, Condon continued. Almost full at six o'clock when the bellboy first saw it, it was now almost empty. "So no wonder he's drunk as a goat," Condon said. "On top of what he had in the bar."

He had one more piece of information on Seymour to report: He'd arrived by car, a Chevvy four or five years old, with Connecticut license plates.

"He's been in town, though, a couple of weeks, I think," Fergus said. "I want to know where he was staying. Try some other hotels, will you?"

The security officer tried other hotels, the three or four good ones first, then a few of the lesser ones. "No dice," he said, looking up from the telephone. "Maybe he stayed in a motel. I'll try them."

The motels in the area gave him negative answers.

"Keep trying," Fergus said. "He didn't roost in a tree."

Condon shrugged and, in descending order, went through the list in the classified section of the telephone directory. He made the calls without putting down the receiver, and the lower he went in the hierarchy of Ridgeway's thirty-odd hotels the more abrupt his voice became.

At the twenty-eighth his eyebrows shot up. "Zatso?" he said into the mouthpiece. "When'd he check in? . . . I see . . . And checked out this morning. Everything kosher? . . . Uh-huh. Okay, thanks a lot."

He hung up and looked at Fergus. "He's been at the Lincoln since Saturday, October 4. Checked out this morning and came here. The Lincoln," he repeated with deep disgust. "I hope to God he didn't bring us bedbugs from that dump."

"Any trouble there?"

"No, kept to himself. Worked somewhere, they thought, what little attention they paid to him. Then this morning he just checked out and came here." Condon shook his head.

"Quite a step up in the world," Fergus said.

"Yeah. Guy'd have to be stony broke to hole up at the Lincoln. We'll have to keep an eye on him. He seems to be throwing money around now, though. He's tipping well, he's bought new clothes and plenty of liquor. Maybe he came into some money. You know, dice, cards, numbers, horses. Or something."

"Yes," Fergus said. "Or something."

Chapter Twelve

It was after eleven the next morning when Seymour awoke, disoriented at first in the unfamiliar room, more luxurious than any he had slept in for years. His burning thirst and nausea told him first of all that he had a hangover. Then he began to piece together where he was and what had taken place yesterday, beginning with the money from Andrea, the purchase of the car, the move to this hotel room, the trip to —

Effie Horbal! Christ above, what did the paper say about her?

He swung his legs over the side of the bed and sat up. The room rocked around him. He had to hold his swimming head in his hands. But his physical condition was the least of his problems. What did the paper say about Effie Horbal?

He staggered to the bathroom, gagged and almost vomited when he tried to quench his thirst with a glass of water. He made his way to the bureau to investigate his supply of bourbon. There were two good drinks left in the bottle. He tossed off the first one and sipped the second a little at a time. He felt better, well enough, after he sat down on the bed, to phone room service and order a large glass of tomato juice, coffee, and a copy of the *Post* sent up.

As soon as the bourbon took hold he couldn't sit still. He walked the floor, worrying about Effie. What a crazy damn fool he'd been, getting drunk last night! For all he knew, the police had been on his trail for hours. He should have stayed cold sober and waited up for the first edition of the paper. If it said one word about Effie that spelled danger to him, he could have taken off immediately and been a couple of hundred miles away by this time.

When the waiter appeared, Seymour barely gave him time to set down the tray before he had signed the check, shoved a tip in his hand, and got him out of the room.

The *Post* lay neatly folded on the tray. Seymour shook it open. Nothing on the front page, his feverish scrutiny told him. So much to the good . . .

He turned the pages, his eyes darting up and down the columns until, at the very back of the first section, he came upon what he was looking for. Headed, OLDFIELD WOMAN KILLED IN FALL, it said that Mrs. Effie Horbal, 45, had been found dead late yesterday afternoon in her isolated farm home at the west end of town. Her body was discovered on the cellar floor by her husband, Walter Horbal, when he returned home from work at 5 P.M. Police theorized that Mrs. Horbal, who rarely had visitors, had been alone in the house and might have suffered from a sudden illness that caused her to fall the full length of the cellar stairs. Her skull had been fractured on the cement floor. Death was believed to have been instantaneous. Sergeant William Krajeski, resident state policeman, was in charge of the investigation.

Seymour sank down on the bed in relief, reached shakily for a cigarette, and poured himself a cup of coffee. He was safe, just as he'd known he would be yesterday. He'd covered himself perfectly. Luck had played some part, of course, in his not being seen on the road from the Horbals', but luck wasn't the main factor. He'd used his head and fooled the police with a perfect murder; not an unsolved one that would remain open on the books, but a perfect murder written off as an accidental death.

Seymour drank two cups of coffee and the tomato juice. He felt like a different person from the man who had stumbled out of bed half an hour ago, hung over and panic-stricken.

He took a shower, put on one of the new

shirts he'd bought yesterday and the slacks and jacket he'd worn last night. When he was dressed he stood at a window, looking down at the street three stories below. He thought about last night. Nothing that had occurred when he met Andrea's father was altogether clear in his memory but he retained the impression that Langdon had snubbed him. But why should he care about an arrogant old bastard like Langdon? He'd change his tune fast if he knew what Seymour knew about his precious daughter. Serve him right, by God, if Seymour told him.

He wouldn't, of course. He had no intention of killing the goose that laid the golden eggs. What an unpleasant surprise it must have been for Andrea, though, when he'd turned up at the dinner last night — if she'd been simple-minded enough to believe that he would get out of Ridgeway, with only coffee money to show for his trouble and leave her free to go on posing as a saint in plaster.

Well, at least she knew better now. She must be going nuts this morning, wondering what was coming next. He wouldn't call her or go near her today. He'd let her stew around and get softened up for the big one while he took a run over to Littleton to see what Langdon wills were on record at city hall. Raising the fifteen hundred she'd given him yesterday had involved no more effort for her than writing a check. No mention had been made of having to account to her father for it. Therefore, it seemed logical to assume she not only had an allowance but also money of her own, inherited from her mother, perhaps, or from her grandparents. He would find out about this in Littleton and while he was there he might as well take a look at the grand list to see if there was an assessment on property in her name.

Before he left for Littleton, though, he'd better give Walt Horbal a ring and catch up on the latest developments in Oldfield.

He lifted the telephone receiver and then dropped it back in place as if it had burned his hand. What was he thinking of? He had to make the call from a pay booth where there'd be no record of it to connect him with the Horbals.

The day looked windy and cold. He'd better take his new topcoat with him. He laid it over his arm, English wool, light and warm and expensive and went downstairs.

It occurred to him in the elevator that he was supposed to be working today. But he was done with Frankie's Handy Lunchroom; why bother to call up and say so? Let Frankie figure it out for himself that he was short one kitchen man. He owed Seymour a day's pay. He could keep it for a consolation prize.

He called Walt from a booth in the lobby. Walt answered the phone himself. He sounded subdued but not in the least suspicious as Seymour told him he'd just read about Effie's death in the paper and what a shock it had given him.

"Well, it sure was a shock to me," Walt said. "The worst I ever had." He went on to relate details of coming home and finding her; the advent of the doctor and state policeman; the fact that they kept only a wood fire in the furnace this time of the year and that she'd probably been going down to check on it when she fell.

"The paper said death was instantaneous."

"Yeah. The doctor said at least I didn't have to worry that she lay there and suffered."

Walt didn't sound as if he would have worried unduly in any case. He sounded subdued but that was all. Presently he said, "And how's our little business deal coming along?"

"Well, I had a talk with the lady and got a small down payment yesterday. I'm going to give her a day or two to think it over before I really move in on her."

"Uh-huh. Well I'm under plenty of expense myself right now. Effie didn't have much insurance and I got to scratch up the rest of the money to bury her."

"When's the funeral?"

"Saturday afternoon. She's got a couple of cousins over Norfolk way. They're going to stay over Saturday night, I guess. It'll be from a funeral parlor in Hotchkissville. And as I was saying, there'll be plenty of expense."

"Well, I can let you have a couple of hundred if that will help."

"You only get four hundred?"

Seymour almost dropped the receiver. Why, the stupid lout thought he was entitled to half! Seymour did all the work, took all the risk but still the stupid lout thought that it was going to be a share-alike deal.

They hadn't had a chance yet to discuss the division of the profits. But this wasn't the moment to bring it up. Seymour said, "I got a little more than that. However—"

"How much?"

How much should he say? Horbal would see that he had a car.

"Seven hundred was what I got," he said. "But I have to have transportation out to your place. I couldn't keep borrowing the heap I was driving so I picked up a car for three hundred. We'll split the rest."

"But you'll still owe me half of what you paid for the car, huh?"

"There is the question of my expenses," Seymour reminded him coldly. "But we needn't go into that now. When shall I come out to see you?"

"Well, Effie's cousins will probably stay all day Sunday. I'll be alone by Monday, though, and I don't figure to go back to work before

Tuesday or Wednesday. So why don't you come out Monday afternoon?"

"All right, I'll see you then."

This was business. No more would be said about Walt's sudden bereavement. He spoke again of Effie's funeral expenses and said he'd need more than two hundred soon. Seymour suggested that they'd better not discuss the matter too freely over the phone, said good-by, and hung up.

"The stupid lout," he fumed to himself as he left the phone booth. "The greedy son of a bitch. He's making the biggest mistake of his life if he thinks he's going to get half of what I get from Andrea. This whole thing was my idea from the beginning. And what's he done to promote it? He's done nothing. He's just sat on his ass over there in Oldfield with not one thing that could be proved against him if Andrea ever started to fight back. And yet he has the nerve to tell me—"

Seymour calmed down over breakfast in the coffee shop. Andrea wouldn't fight back. She'd pay and she'd go on paying; she'd let him wring every cent she had out of her before she'd let anything about the kid become public property.

In Littleton he'd find out what she had, how much she could afford to pay.

Chapter Thirteen

All that day, Thursday, while her father was off on a street-corner campaign, Andrea kept to her room. She didn't feel well, she said, and could take no calls or see anyone.

Her statement wasn't far from the truth. She wasn't physically ill except for a feeling of exhaustion; but emotionally she was ill from a burden of guilt and sorrow carried too long alone. Seymour's reappearance in her life, his demands, her fresh fears of exposure, the fresh lies she had to tell, and above all, the dreadful pretense she had to keep up that Greg was still alive — these were a burden almost too great to be borne. But no matter how her mind twisted and turned seeking a way out, there was none she could find. Anger, hatred of Seymour were no use at all; had never been any use.

She lay in bed, not reading or sleeping, doing

nothing except to look out the window at white cloud puffs blown across the sky by the wind and tell herself tiredly that if she could just shut her eyes and never open them again in life it would be best for her and best for her father. He would grieve over losing her, yes; but he would be left with his illusions intact; he would remember his daughter as a good and honest person.

Nothing was that easy, though. She couldn't shut her eyes and never open them again. She had been living a lie for ten years and now she had to face the fact that it was closing in on her, that she had no more control over her life than the clouds in the sky in the presence of the wind. The control of her life since the night of *Program Personality* had rested with Seymour and the Horbals.

She did not read the paper that morning.

Fergus called and left the message that he hoped she'd soon feel better. He didn't believe what the maid said on the phone about her illness—Andrea's, he felt, was of the spirit—but he could be held off by it, hampered as he was by good manners and consideration of her right to privacy if that was what she wanted.

Her father, too, returning home late in the day to shower and change for a dinner meeting, could be held off with the story that she felt overtired, seemed to have a cold coming on, and was spending the day in bed. When he looked in on her she pretended to be asleep.

But the next morning Seymour couldn't be held off. He gave his name to the maid and said, "Please tell Miss Langdon it's important that I talk with her immediately."

Andrea took the call in her room. She was a cloud puff he could blow in whatever direction he chose.

"I'm so sorry you're not feeling well," he said solicitously when she came on the line. "But something's turned up that means I really must see you today. I had thought we might meet here in town but as long as you're ill I'd better come out to the house. What time would be best for you?"

She couldn't allow him ever again to come to the house. "I'm not that ill," she said in a voice dead to feeling. "I'd prefer to meet you in town. The restaurant where we met Wednesday will do. I'll be there at eleven o'clock."

Eleven o'clock was only an hour away. She might have set a later time for their appointment but she saw no gain in postponing the inevitable. It was better to find out right away what the next turn of the screw was to be.

When she went into the restaurant she found Seymour there ahead of her, seated in the booth farthest away from the few people who were present at that in-between hour. He stood up to greet her with his fox's grin silken smooth and beckoned the waitress to order coffee for her, overriding Andrea's refusal of it with the statement, "We'll be here awhile."

He took charge of the conversation. He told her he'd meant to leave Wednesday as he'd said he would but instead, he'd had a few drinks to celebrate his fresh start in life and ended up taking one over the eight — otherwise, he'd never have appeared at the dinner for her father. "After all," he added earnestly, "it's been no part of my intention to embarrass you in public, Andrea."

Yesterday, he continued, he'd gone to Oldfield to give the Horbals their share of the money — he watched her narrowly as he said this, but Andrea's still face showed no change; apparently the newspaper account of Effie's death had escaped her notice — and while he was there something new had come up. . . .

He threw this statement away, letting his voice drift off into silence.

Andrea offered no comment. She merely waited, her gaze on the untouched cup of coffee in front of her.

When he realized she wasn't going to ask him what had come up, that he was to be deprived of that last measure of satisfaction — which was due him, he thought, considering the superior manner she and her father displayed toward him — he dropped the mask of courtesy abruptly. "Why didn't you tell me Greg was dead?" The question came out like the lash of a whip.

167

He had broken through her aloofness at last. Her face turned ashen in its pallor. He thought she was going to faint.

"For God's sake—" He picked up a glass of water and thrust it at her. "Drink it."

She had to use both hands to hold the glass. At first she couldn't swallow. Then she drained it.

Seymour studied her. She looked a little better now. He had hit her too hard and too fast. It had been a near thing that she hadn't fainted on him. Life had always been too easy for her, that was her trouble. The one problem she'd ever had to cope with was the kid, and she'd had money enough to keep him tucked away out of sight; and then, conveniently for her, very conveniently, he'd died in the fire. She'd got away with having an illegitimate child; she could still hold her head as high as if he'd never existed. As for Seymour, he was the kid's father but she didn't give a damn about him. She'd been only too eager to pay him off with a few dollars and keep everything swept under the rug.

The thought of his position compared to hers brought hot resentment that had to be kept to himself. She couldn't take it. She couldn't take anything.

He said, "It changes everything. Up until yesterday I thought Greg was alive," the lie came effortlessly, "and I didn't want to hurt him, my own kid. I was ready to accept a small pay-off and go away. But yesterday I got talking to the Horbals—I'd read the story in the *Post* that said you were in the Broome's Cove fire, and they told me you had Greg with you the day it happened . . ."

He went on to tell her that when he returned from Oldfield yesterday he went to the *POST*, read about the fire, and saw the pictures of Greg. "The Horbals have snapshots of him," he added. "There's no question but that it was the same kid. So it's no use denying it."

Andrea didn't deny it. She was silent.

He adopted a righteous tone. "What you chose to tell the Horbals was one thing; but to pretend to me, the kid's own father, that he was alive and well— How could you do it, Andrea?"

She was silent, her eyes enormous with strain.

"I wouldn't put anything past a woman who'd pull a stunt like that," he said next. "I'll bet it was a big relief to you when you found out the kid was dead. You didn't have to worry about hiding him away any more. You thought you were safe forever, the rich, proper Miss Langdon with the rich, proper father."

He dropped his righteous tone and turned brisk. "You didn't even bring a suit although you could have got quite a settlement. You didn't need it, of course, but I'm not so lucky as you. I've got nothing. I could use a settlement from the insurance company. It might pay me to have a lawyer look into it. He could at

169

least tell me what the statute of limitations is on it."

This was too much. Andrea said quietly, "You have no case. You can't prove you were Greg's father. You saw to it that he didn't bear your name." She paused. "I'm glad of that now. It's the only thing I have to be glad about."

His face darkened. He abandoned for good all pretense of regret for the past as he drawled, "How long did you wait that day for me to show up with a marriage license in my hand?"

Thank God you never did. This was a thought to keep to herself. Recriminations would serve no purpose but to add to her shame.

Seymour said, "I don't know what my rights are. I can find out, though. I can go to a lawyer, go to the police, at least get the kid identified. Buried under a number! Little Sir 915. Don't you lie awake nights thinking about it?" He brooded aloud, "I wonder if there's a charge they'd bring against you for not identifying him. I don't see what it would be myself but there might be one."

Andrea looked at him with revulsion. "I give you money and you say you'll go. But you don't. Will you never go?"

"If you make it worth my while. So far all I've had from you is coffee money. But if I had enough, do you think I'd hang around a graveyard like Ridgeway? I'd go to Florida or the Caribbean and have myself a little fun for the

170

first time in years. In fact, I'd get out of here so fast you wouldn't see my dust. Of course there'd have to be a final payment to the Horbals too. They'd probably go back to Nevada and then you'd have us all off your hands."

He meant it this time. If she gave him enough money, she could buy herself a respite from him until it was gone. Then he would be back for more. And more. It would go on without end.

But even though she knew no protest would help her she said, "Are you trying to force me to take this to my father?"

Seymour shrugged. "That's up to you. He'd want it kept quiet too. Your money, his money, it doesn't matter which to me. Not that you need his. I've done a little checking in Littleton, you see. Your mother left you plenty. A profitable business block free of all encumbrances and a nice collection of stocks and bonds. Take fifty thousand out of it and you still won't be on relief. That includes the Horbals' share. You'll have nothing to worry about where they're concerned, once I've paid them off. I realize, of course, that you can't get that much together overnight." His tone indicated that he thought he was being very reasonable in his attitude. "I'm prepared to give you a full week. That is, until a week from today. If you can get it sooner, naturally I'll be on my way sooner."

Andrea looked at him for a moment in silence. Then she said, "I can't get it at all, not that much. The bank in Littleton would make a fuss and bring it to my father's attention and he'd—" Her voice died away as Seymour broke in to say sharply, "That's your problem. Solve it your way. But fifty thousand is the figure I've set and if you offer me less I'll be back for the rest of it. Once I get it I give you my word you'll never hear from me again. Or from the Horbals who wouldn't dare make a move without me."

His word wasn't worth the breath it took to give it. He was a hollow man. There was nothing inside him, nothing to appeal to, nothing to reach. She stood up to go. Without looking at him she said, "I'll have to see what I can do."

"A week from today," Seymour said. "I'll give you until three when the banks close and I'll meet you here. Small bills, no larger than twenties. On second thought, you might as well include some fifties so there won't be so much bulk."

She didn't answer. She left him standing by the booth. Outside the restaurant she walked fast, almost ran to her car in her need to put distance between Seymour and her.

But on the way home revulsion had to yield to the realities of her situation, the fact that she must raise fifty thousand dollars in cash in a week's time. There was only one course open to her. She would have to go to Littleton today to see someone at her bank about it. Why not leave a note for her father and spend the weekend there? If she did that and stayed quietly at a hotel, she'd avoid having to see anyone; and sometime Monday—how long did these things take?—perhaps she could complete whatever arrangements had to be made for taking out a mortgage on the business block her mother had left her. Above all, she had to give careful thought to what she was going to say at the bank. Otherwise, they'd get in touch with her father.

While the surface of Andrea's mind was occupied with immediate plans, beneath the surface revulsion lingered and consuming shame. A week from today she had to pay fifty thousand dollars to a man who was in a position to blackmail her because he was Greg's father. Nothing could ever erase or change that fact in any way. He was the father of her adorable little boy. How many times since that New Year's Eve ten years ago she'd gone over and over that night and its aftermath, not trying to excuse herself but wondering how she could have been so dazzled by Seymour that only a month after they'd met she had thrown away the precepts of a lifetime for him.

No use to say how young she was, not eighteen until the end of the month, and so totally unaccustomed to drinking that what she'd had that night might well be taken into account. No

173

excuses, no palliation . . .

But later on, driving to Littleton, she wondered bleakly why her one lapse from virtue had had to involve her with a man without scruple, a drunken sadist, a blackmailer. Wasn't she paying heavily enough for her long-ago madness without that weight added to the payment?

It took effort to remind herself that no weight she carried could restore Greg's life to him.

Chapter Fourteen

Fergus called Andrea that afternoon not long after she left for Littleton and was told she had gone out of town and wouldn't be back before Monday at the earliest. He had little time that weekend to think about her. With the political campaign moving into its last fortnight and candidates making speeches all over the state, he was kept busy analyzing their chances in two Sunday features as well as the daily stories he wrote.

Monday brought a lull, a respite for candidate and voter, with no major political events scheduled. Fergus was at his desk early in the day and, in the relative quiet of the city room at that hour, wrote what he regarded with satisfaction as a good solid piece on Connecticut's drift toward the Democratic Party since 1930. By eleven o'clock he was finished and immediately his hand moved toward the telephone to call Andrea. He drew it back, eying it severely as if it had been guilty of independent action for which he bore no responsibility. Give her a margin of time to get home, he thought; don't hound her day and night.

He sat back in his chair, lit a cigarette, and turned his thoughts to Seymour Boyd.

Was he still registered at the Wilton? There were two ways to find out: pick up the phone or inquire in person.

Fergus decided on the latter course. He'd have a talk with the security officer on duty and find out if anything new had come to light since he'd focused the staff's attention on Boyd the other night.

He drove to the hotel and started to go in by way of the coffee shop, the nearest entrance from the parking lot. But he was no sooner through the door than he ducked back out to avoid coming face to face with Seymour, who was heading toward him from the desk where he had just paid for a meal. Seymour, putting change in his pocket, didn't see him. By the time he came out the door, Fergus had propped himself against the building, whisked a copy of the *Post* out of his pocket, and had it spread open in front of him, taking a small-boy enjoyment in employing this traditional device of the cloak-and-dagger trade.

Seymour passed him without a glance and

went on to the parking lot.

Why not follow him? Fergus thought. Just to see what he did with himself.

Keeping his distance, he reached his car, got into it, and watched the attendant shift two cars before Seymour could get into his.

It was the Chevvy Condon had mentioned and although it was four or five years old it was a vast improvement on what he had been driving last week and could be taken as another sign of increased prosperity.

When Seymour drove out of the parking lot, Fergus followed him. In the congested downtown area where he could easily lose him, he had to keep closer than he liked; but apparently it didn't enter Seymour's mind that he was being followed. The heavy traffic engaged his full attention until they were out of the city. After that Fergus dropped back, a little at first and then still more when it became clear that for the present, at least, Seymour meant to keep to the main highway they were now on.

They were traveling northeast. After they crossed the Connecticut River there was little traffic on the route they took. Seymour maintained a steady fifty, the posted speed limit, and Fergus, just keeping the Chevvy in sight, maintained the same speed.

At two-thirty they came into Oldfield. Fergus couldn't recall ever having been there before and after his first glimpse of the center didn't care if he never came again.

He was getting hungrier by the minute. Boyd had eaten just before setting out but he'd had nothing to eat since his eight-thirty breakfast. He was not only hungry but he also wondered if he was making a fool of himself. This could be the most innocent of outings and here he was, perhaps wasting the best part of a day when there were many better things he might have been doing with it.

How much farther were they going, anyway?

He had dropped far back on the secondary road to Oldfield where other cars were almost a rarity. A few miles beyond the center he was so far behind that he came close to losing the other car when it went around a curve and took a left-hand road. The sign on it said Hotchkissville, a textile town of which Fergus had some knowledge.

But Hotchkissville wasn't their destination, he learned shortly, when he came to the crest of a hill just in time to see the Chevvy swing off on another road to the right. At the foot of the hill he slowed down and eyed it in surprise. It was a gravel road that looked as if it saw little use and went nowhere, not the sort of road he would expect Seymour Boyd, allegedly a newcomer to the state, to have business on.

Fergus turned off on it, moving at a crawl, not knowing what to look for and, above all, not wanting to come upon the other man parked unexpectedly around the next curve. He passed a deserted farmhouse and then no other dwelling place for some distance. There was no indication that anyone else lived on the road until he heard faintly the slam of a car door ahead. He braked to a stop, got out of his car, leaving the door open, and took cover in under-brush before he looked around the curve in front of him.

He saw a weather-beaten old farmhouse ahead on his right. The Chevvy was parked in the driveway, and Seymour was speaking to a coarse-looking, middle-aged man who had come out of the house to greet him. From where he stood Fergus could read the name "Walter Horbal" painted on the mailbox at the edge of the road.

The two men stood talking in the driveway for a minute or so. Although their voices carried on the still air, Fergus wasn't close enough to catch more than a few words here and there. Boyd was sorry about something. Whatever it was, the older man said it had knocked him for a loop. Then Boyd said something about going inside. The other shook his head and moved toward a bench set against the wall of the house. Boyd raised an objection; the other spoke so sharply that every word of it reached Fergus. "It's nice out here in the sun," he said. "House gives me the willies since I came home and found Effie the other day."

179

Boyd sat down beside him.

Now they were a good fifteen or twenty feet farther away from Fergus and seemed to have lowered their voices to speak confidentially. He could no longer hear a word they said but he had to stay where he was; no nearer cover was available to him.

Minutes went by. The other man — Horbal? — did most of the talking at first, Boyd nodding from time to time and looking sympathetic. Then it was his turn to talk. For a brief period an argument seemed to be going on, with Boyd apparently getting the better of it or at least overriding the other man's remarks. Presently, after a quick glance around, he took out his wallet, extracted a number of bills, and handed them to the other man who counted them carefully before he put them in his pocket. More conversation followed; then Boyd stood up and moved toward his car with the plain intent of leaving.

Fergus hurried back to his car. He could only hope that the pair in the driveway would be too absorbed in what they said to hear the sound of the motor. He didn't shut the door or take the time to turn around where he was. He backed his car all the way to the deserted farmhouse, drove up the weed-grown driveway, and parked in back of the house out of sight. He had more of a wait for the Chevvy than he'd anticipated. Boyd and the other man must have found they had more things to talk about before Boyd left.

When the other car finally passed the house, Fergus waited another two or three minutes before he drove away himself. He had no thought of trying to catch up with Seymour, taking it for granted that he had completed his business in Oldfield and would head back to Ridgeway. Fergus's immediate concerns were getting something to eat and seeking information on Walter Horbal.

He drove back to Oldfield. He hadn't noticed the "Resident State Policeman" sign in front of one of the houses when he went through the center earlier; but this time his attention was drawn to it by the state-police car in the yard. He decided he could go without food a little longer and stopped his car in front of the house.

The police officer answered the door himself. He was in uniform, with a sergeant's chevrons on his sleeve, a trim, graying man with an erect carriage and a competent air. Fergus introduced himself and took out his press card.

The officer said, "Come in, Mr. MacDonald. I'm Sergeant Krajeski." He led the way across the hall to his office. "What can I do for you?" he asked when they were seated.

"I'm looking for information on a man named Walter Horbal," Fergus told him. "He lives a few miles out although I suppose it's within the town limits." He went on to describe the house and the man he had seen there.

"Yes, that's the place and it sounds like Horbal. I've known who he was but until the other day—" He paused and raised an eyebrow. "I never knew him to be in politics in any way." He smiled. "You can see I get the *Post*, Mr. MacDonald. I'm one of your regular readers."

"Oh." Fergus returned his smile. "Let's hope it's not going to be prejudicial to my inquiries."

The sergeants smile broadened. "It won't be."

"Good. Now, about Mr. Horbal—"

The police officer gave no sign that he had noticed Fergus still kept to himself the reason for his interest in Walt Horbal. He took out his pipe and got it filled and lit before he said, "There's not too much I can tell you about him. He works at the mill in Hotchkissville and doesn't show up around here very often. He's not a man you'd take to right off. I'd never paid much attention to him until I got the call to go out there the other day when his wife died. That's the first time I ever really tried to size him up."

"His wife died and you were called in on it?" Fergus looked startled but only for a moment. Thinking back to the scene at the farmhouse, the suspicions he already held regarding Seymour, the confidential talk, the money changing hands, it came as no great surprise to him that the manner of Mrs. Horbal's death should lead to a police investigation. "I didn't know Mrs.

182

Horbal had just died," he said. "For that matter, I didn't know there was a Mrs. Horbal. What happened to her?"

Sergeant Krajeski gave him a résumé of Effie's death. Then he said, "According to Dr. West, she'd been dead not more than three or four hours and not less than two when he first saw her, which means she died sometime between one and three. At that time—and I checked on it carefully—Horbal was at work. He had a few beers after work and didn't get home until five. If you've seen the place you know there are no neighbors to come forward with information. And Mrs. Horbal, from what I've found out, had very few visitors. She was a woman who had little to say and hardly ever went out, so she must have led a pretty isolated life."

He puffed on his pipe for an interval. Then he said, "There was nothing out of the way, no indication of a visitor, no signs of foul play. In the absence of all evidence to the contrary, it has to go down as an accidental death."

"Um," said Fergus. His mind already bristling with suspicions of Seymour, he took another look at last Wednesday afternoon. He knew nothing of Seymour's whereabouts then; he only knew that he had changed hotels in the morning and turned up drunk in the Wilton ballroom in the evening. Today he had driven to hell and gone out here to pay a visit to the newly-made

183

widower who didn't look at all like his cup of tea and had given him money. Would it do any good almost a week later to have Condon ask around at the Wilton if anyone remembered seeing Boyd in the hotel that afternoon between one and three?

Well, that would be reaching out into the wild blue yonder. But still, he'd ask Condon to do it.

The sergeant watched him, taking note of the concentrated, inward-looking expression he wore. Presently he said, "What's your interest in Horbal and his wife's death, Mr. MacDonald? It's certainly not political."

It was time for Fergus to lay some of his cards—although none that brought Andrea into the picture—on the table. "No, it's not political," he replied. "There's a man in Ridgeway, a shady character, I've had my eye on. I followed him today. He went to see Horbal . . ." Fergus proceeded to tell the sergeant what had taken place between Seymour and Walt Horbal. He added emphatically that he could think of no bond of friendship or business association existing between two such disparate types, one of them supposed to be a newcomer to the state.

"So that's my interest in Horbal," he concluded. "And now you tell me his wife died just the other day under questionable circumstances. Did she have a heart condition or any kind of sickness that might have brought on her fall?"

"Well . . ." The sergeant hesitated. "She'd

184

started menopause, her doctor said. That sometimes leads to dizzy spells in women. If she'd been having them, though, she hadn't mentioned it to her husband." He hesitated again. "To tell you the truth, I'm not too happy about the whole thing. But with her husband in the clear and no one else involved, what can you call it except an accidental death?"

"Um," Fergus said and then, "I didn't care much for Horbal's looks."

The sergeant settled deeper in his chair, sucked on his pipe, and said, "There's been a lot of talk about him around here since Mrs. Horbal's death. People liked her well enough but no one seems to have a good word for her husband. The talk that went on when they came back from Nevada last spring has all been revived again."

"Talk about what?"

"Mrs. Horbal's inheritance. God knows what it actually amounted to—you can't tell from all the talk you hear—but anyway, there was an inheritance from a relative in Nevada about four years ago and they went out there at the time. They didn't try to sell the farm, though—it belonged to Mrs. Horbal—just closed it up and left, although I heard yesterday that there was some arrangement made with a man in Hotchkissville to go over once in a while and check on things. But people around here thought they'd gone for good. Then last spring they came back and there was a lot of talk about Horbal gambling away his wife's inheritance. Everyone seemed to believe it because they didn't have much use for him and knew that he'd always bullied her and had her right under his thumb. He got his old job back at the mill and they kept to themselves more than ever, as if they were ashamed, people said, of coming back with their tails between their legs. But everyone felt sorry for her. She was a nice woman."

There was nothing in this for Fergus except that Walt Horbal might be in need of money. "Any children?" he asked.

"No, never had any of their own. But back before they went away they had a youngster boarding with them, a child they got through answering an ad in the paper. At least that's what I seem to remember hearing at the time. I was new in town then."

"How old was the child?" Fergus couldn't have said himself why he asked the question, pursued the matter at all.

"Oh, I think they had him from babyhood until they went to Nevada. But the only time I ever remember seeing him was some years back when I drove out past their place to check on a power line that went down in a storm. It's not a road you'd patrol regularly, you know. But this particular day the child was playing in the front yard when I went by. He was probably two or three years old at the time. A cute little red-headed fellow."

A redheaded little boy; a redheaded man. Fergus tried to sound casual as he asked, "What became of him when the Horbals left?"

Sergeant Krajeski looked surprised at this continuing interest in the child. He said, "Well, I guess whoever was boarding him there took him away at the time. But what's he—?"

The unfinished question hung in the air while Fergus hesitated over his answer. For some reason still far from clear to him he wasn't prepared to link the child with Seymour just yet.

While he hesitated, the police officer took the choice away from him. His surprised look vanished as he said on a ruminating note, "A couple of days ago Mrs. Miller at the store down the road was talking about the Horbals and she mentioned that some man had been in inquiring about them not long ago. He said a friend of his was a friend of theirs. He was tall and nicely dressed and had a very gentlemanly manner, Mrs. Miller said." The sergeant's glance turned quizzical. "He also had red hair." The sergeant paused. "What's this all about, Mr. MacDonald?"

"I honestly don't know," Fergus told him. "I'd never heard of the child until you mentioned him. I can't see where he fits in. Maybe he doesn't. Red hair's not so uncommon. But the man I followed from Ridgeway has red hair. He

187

must be the same one. I don't know what he's up to. All I really know about him so far is that he's a shady character. And now you tell me there's a red-haired child." He sighed in bewilderment. "Can you find out exactly when the Horbals went to Nevada? Maybe it's a starting point, maybe not."

"Easy enough to check on." The sergeant reached for the phone on the desk. "The light-company office in Hotchkissville will tell me when the service was disconnected." He dialed a number, asked to speak to Mr. Putnam, got him on the line, and after a few preliminaries stated his reason for calling. There was a waiting period before the light-company man came back to the phone. The sergeant listened, thanked him, and hung up. "The service was disconnected September 25, 1954," he informed Fergus. "We can take it as the date the Horbals left."

"Yes . . ." Fergus realized that the date had no special significance for the sergeant, who lived in a different part of the state and wasn't a newspaperman who had covered the Broome's Cove fire on September 25, 1954 . . . Although what, Fergus asked himself, did that have to do with the Horbals or Seymour Boyd?

Deep within himself he knew, obscurely, the answer. Already he had moved on to the fact that Andrea was injured in the fire.

He kept all this to himself and stayed a few minutes longer, turning the conversation back to

Effie Horbal's death He asked the sergeant to let him know if he heard anything more about the redheaded man or Walt Horbal. Then he expressed his thanks, shook hands, and left.

His mind was so filled with conjecture that he was out of the house before he remembered that Little Sir 915 had been a redhead.

Chapter Fifteen

That same afternoon Andrea sat in the vice-president's office at her bank in Littleton, conferring over the papers drawn to mortgage the business block she owned. The vice-president, who had known her since childhood, continued to exude disapproval of the whole transaction, as he had from the moment of her arrival at the bank on Friday. The reason she gave for taking out the mortgage—a friend going into business, she putting up capital as a silent partner, the details still a highly secret matter—hadn't, of course, come within miles of satisfying the vice-president. But it was the best she could think of; there just wasn't, so far as she was concerned, a plausible reason for suddenly needing fifty thousand dollars.

The vice-president had been shocked as well as disapproving. He had tried to insist on an investigation of the mythical friend's background and financial resources and proposed new product. He had delivered a long lecture on the risk involved, the percentage of bankruptcies in new businesses, the sanctity of capital, the inadvisability of mixing business with friendship, and so on.

When he had found Andrea firm in her intent, he had told her he couldn't approve the mortgage without first consulting her father. She'd been ready for that with a tactful but firm reminder that she was twenty-seven years old and the owner of the property, with the right to do whatever she thought best with it. Her father, she'd said, couldn't possibly be approached on the matter now; his campaign kept him on the run day and night. "There'll be time for me to discuss it with him after the election," she'd said, her embarrassment and distress buried deep under an air of candor.

"Before you sign anything that commits you to this project?"

"Yes," she had replied, "before I sign one thing."

This assurance had mollified the vice-president a little. Eventually he had sent for someone from the mortgage department to initiate the transaction; and now, Monday afternoon, Andrea sat in his office waiting to sign the mortgage papers.

The vice-president made one more effort to persuade her to change her mind. He meant well. She kept reminding herself of that. It helped her to endure the long harassment. She signed here and here as he indicated and at last it was done.

Not quite done, however. Once again he brought her father into it, "Now you promise you'll talk to your father about it as soon as the election is over and before you've committed yourself?"

"I won't sign a thing without consulting him," Andrea replied, trying to find some comfort in this ambiguity which wasn't quite as full-bodied a lie as everything else she had said to the paternally inclined vice-president. But no real comfort or self-deception was possible. It was a web of lies, every word of it. Her whole life was a web of lies and had been for years.

"We'll mail you the check before the week is out," the vice-president told her in a dissatisfied tone, consistent to the very end in not approving of one bit of it.

She couldn't press him for a check made out on the spot, not when she'd said she wasn't going to invest the money until after the election. But this was only Monday. Before the week was out meant before the Friday deadline. She would just have to resign herself to the fact that she couldn't pay off Seymour ahead of time and get him out of Ridgeway.

She left the bank and Littleton as fast as she could and arrived home in time to welcome her father back from a day of campaigning. For his

benefit she put on gaiety with the dress she
changed into for dinner and afterward helped
him entertain a group of High Point Volunteers
for Langdon. Her eyes and cheeks were bright.
No one who watched her working on changes in
the voting list would have thought she had a
care in the world beyond getting her father
elected to Congress.

At bedtime she told him she'd accompany
him on a round of coffee hours tomorrow in
Eastham, a town at the other end of the county.
She felt fine after her nice, restful weekend, she
said. She'd got over her cold completely.

She went to bed and lay awake counting the
hours left until Friday afternoon at three. This
time Seymour would go. After he had made his
sordid division of the spoils with the Horbals
they and he would go.

He would be back, though, when he had
spent what she would give him Friday. This she
could be sure of; this was her future prospect to
which her thoughts must return again and
again.

She didn't allow herself to think of Fergus.
She had almost given herself away to him the
other night when he had come to her rescue at
the Wilton and then offered to help her. Tonight
his name had been on the list of people who
had called while she was in Littleton. But it was
no use to call him back. The more she saw him,
the more she fell in love with him and that led
nowhere. She could never tell him, never tell

193

anyone about Greg. She had kept it to herself, guarded it as she would her life, this far along the road; she would keep it to herself the rest of the way.

When Andrea fell asleep she began to dream. She dreamed she walked along an unfamiliar street in an unfamiliar town and went into a house she had never seen before. It was vague and formless in the dream, with none of the furnishings clearly seen. She wandered through it without purpose until at last she entered an empty, shadowy room and closed the door after her. No one was in the room, no tangible thing menaced her, but little by little it became a terrible and frightening place. She had to get out. She ran back and forth searching for the door by which she had entered. She couldn't find it. Whenever she caught a glimpse of it, the shadows would deepen and it would vanish. As her frenzy mounted, awareness of Fergus came into the dream. He was somewhere close by. If she could only let him know where she was he would find the door and get out of this terrible room. She tried to call his name but no sound came from her lips. She had lost the power of speech. The anguish and frustration of trying to regain it and call his name brought her upright in bed, wide awake, tears running down her face.

Chapter Sixteen

Fergus had his own ordeal to go through that day. He drove back from Oldfield so lost to his surroundings that afterward he had little recollection of the trip, so forgetful of his hunger that he didn't stop for a meal until he was almost in Ridgeway and then ate without appetite or interest in what was set before him. He tried not to believe what his very bones knew to have the inexorable truth of an algebraic equation. X was Andrea, injured in the fire at the Broome's Cove Fair, saying she had attended it alone (But who would attend a fair alone?); Y was Boyd, a drunken no-good who had suddenly appeared from God knew where to blackmail Andrea; X plus Y equaled Little Sir 915, their illegitimate son.

Fergus's heart at first rejected what his mind told him: that the delicately aloof Andrea, with her fastidious manner, had gone to bed with Boyd and borne him a son while hidden away somewhere, employing all sorts of devious devices to hide the truth. She had boarded the child with the Horbals — what name and parentage had been provided for him on his birth certificate? — never admitted his existence, and left him in their care until the very day they were ready to start for Nevada. Then Andrea had taken her son to the fair (although taking him there didn't quite fit into his bitter reconstruction of Andrea as a mother) and, somehow, finding out he was dead before she had to claim him, she had decided not to claim him at all but to take refuge in silence. These were the things she had done.

No lily maid of Astolat was Andrea. She was a girl who had got into trouble with a no-good who, in all likelihood, had walked out on her (not knowing about the Langdon money?). Unlike most girls in her predicament, Andrea had been in a financial position to handle her problem without recourse to a home for unmarried mothers. That much squalidness had been spared her.

It seemed reasonable to assume that she hadn't see Boyd all these years; that his arrival in Ridgeway coincided with the change that had taken place in her after her first date with Fergus; that since Boyd appeared on the scene he had been getting money out of Andrea; that he hadn't known the whole story in the beginning but after becoming acquainted with the Horbals had gone to the *Post* library to check on it.

What a bastard, what an utter bastard he was!

Bastard—illegitimate child. Andrea had borne one. Fergus, slumped at the wheel of his car, scowled blackly at the road ahead.

What pleasure there would be in killing Seymour Boyd with his bare hands!

But by the time he reached Ridgeway the first shock of discovery, with its bitterness and disillusionment, had begun to wear off. Maturer reflection replaced it. He put dates together. Andrea, at school in Washington, had been very young at the time, no more than eighteen. As for Seymour Boyd—was he attractive when he was ten years younger? Grudgingly, Fergus supposed so, although it was impossible for him to see the man through a woman's eyes and certainly not now, ten years later, with the record of his life and character written so plainly on his face that even a child could read it. But Fergus must assume, in fact he knew, that Seymour had been attractive enough to seduce the eighteen-year-old Andrea. Then when he had got her pregnant, he had walked out on her. He couldn't have known about the Langdon money or he would have married her. Now, ten years later, he had found out who she was and how particularly vulnerable she was to blackmail right at this time when the threat of a scandal that would hurt her father's bid for office would terrify her.

What a scandal it would be, too, Fergus

thought next. Andrea Langdon, with her social standing, her father's prominence, the unmarried mother of Little Sir 915, hidden away all his short life and his body unclaimed after the fire at the Broome's Cove Fair which she said she had attended alone.

But why, in the first place, had she taken her son to the fair that day? She might easily have been seen there with him by someone she knew. Fergus thought about this. She must have had some story ready; since she could no longer leave her son with the Horbals it might even have been based on a plan that brought him openly into her life at last.

He was in Ridgeway. He turned down the street to his office, parked in back of the building, and went into it by a side door. His bitter, disillusioned mood had softened to the point of making comparisons. After all, he reminded himself as he rode up in the elevator to the third floor, he was no kid in the throes of calf love; he was getting on toward the middle thirties and hadn't led the life of a saint himself. What right had he to cast stones at Andrea? She'd had a tough break; she was a classic example of the woman who paid. She'd been just a kid taken in by a worthless bastard.

Fergus could think the word bastard now without flinching. Even so, his dark face wore a forbidding expression as he got off the elevator at the third floor and headed for the library. There was nothing in what he had learned today to put him in a pleasant frame of mind.

A different attendant was on duty tonight. Without preliminary conversation Fergus asked for the folder on Little Sir 915 and sat down at a table with it.

He gave his attention first to the two pictures of the dead child. In the light of what he now knew he thought he could trace in the child's round face and unformed features a slight resemblance, or perhaps it was only the promise of resemblance, to the man who was his father.

When he laid the pictures aside there was no vestige of doubt in his mind as to the child's identity.

He turned to the description of the clothing and the polkadot dog, and then to the *Post*'s anniversary stories on the Broome's Cove police officer who was still trying to identify the child. He had read before but he read again about the lines of inquiry pursued, the theories developed, the letters answered from people in all parts of the country; and how none of this had brought the child's identity closer to discovery than it was when the small body was first carried into the Broome's Cove improvised morgue.

Fergus could accept Andrea's failure to claim her son's body now that he was in a calmer, more reflective mood. She was injured and suffering from shock when she found out her son was dead. She hadn't felt equal to what she would have had to face if she came forward. She had taken the easier course of silence; and how many could say that in her position they wouldn't have done the same?

Fergus's thoughts moved on to the Horbals. They had left for Nevada the day of the fire. It seemed likely to him that they had known nothing about their foster child's death all the years they were out of the state; in fact, not until Boyd sought them out in Oldfield. (How he had got on to them was a question to be set aside for the moment as of minor importance.) The blackmail scheme, it seemed, had not originated with them, but they were essential to it, presumably the only people, except Andrea, who could positively identify the dead child. Today he had seen Boyd hand over money to Walter Horbal, who was at least a silent partner in the blackmail scheme, ready to take his cut.

What about Mrs. Horbal, though, who had lived under her bullying husband's thumb? People had considered her a nice woman; Andrea must have had confidence in her or she wouldn't have entrusted her child to her care.

There was no way of knowing how Mrs. Horbal had felt about the blackmail scheme. She was dead. If she'd objected to it, conveniently dead, you might say.

Fergus picked up the phone and called Condon at the Wilton. The security officer informed him that 318—Seymour—hadn't checked out today but was still a guest. He'd been doing a fair amount of drinking off and on in the bar but not since his first night at the hotel had it been necessary for anyone to pour him into bed. He'd made no phone calls from his room although he'd been noticed once or twice using a phone booth in the lobby. He'd had no visitors, received no mail. He was a generous tipper.

That was about all Condon had to offer. Fergus asked him to please find out if any of the hotel staff remembered seeing Seymour in the hotel last Wednesday, the day he registered, between 1 and 3 P.M.

"Jesus, what d'you suspect the guy of, anyway?" Condon's bored sigh reached Fergus clearly over the wire. "He rob a bank or something?"

"That's what I'm trying to find out," Fergus told him.

"Well . . . I'll see what I can do."

"Thanks a lot. Is it all right if I call you about it at noon tomorrow?"

"Yeah, I guess so. But say, if there's a reward out for him I'll expect my cut."

"Of course," Fergus replied.

He hung up. But he did not get much done that night on a follow-up story for next Sunday's paper on the indications of Republican losses in previously unreported areas of the state.

He made no attempt to reach Andrea. Her father was scheduled to speak at a rally in Eastham tomorrow night at which the Republican candidate for governor would make a brief appearance. Rallies were not Fergus's forte but he thought he would attend this one. Andrea would probably be there with her father. It would give him a chance to see her.

He settled himself more firmly in his chair and tried to take an interest in what he was writing. Election Day, after all, was only two weeks away.

Chapter Seventeen

Fergus had Condon on the phone at noon the next day and was told that none of the staff remembered seeing Seymour Boyd around the hotel last Wednesday afternoon.

"Not that it means a lot, one way or the other," Condon added. "It's almost a week ago, and it wasn't until you asked me about him that night that they began to keep an eye on him."

"What about the bellhop who reported the bourbon and the new clothes and so on? And what about the maid who does his room?"

"She says the first time she laid eyes on him was the next day. In the bar they tell me he tied one on early, starting about half past six that night. That was the first time they remember seeing him. So far as I can find out, he's unaccounted for from the time he took the room in the morning until the bellhop carried up the boxes from Schaefer's around six. Then, from six-thirty on, he spent most of the night in the bar. Since you started asking about him, it's a different story, of course. He can't blow his nose without someone noticing it."

It was negative evidence but there it was. Boyd had registered at the Wilton last Wednesday in the forenoon and nobody in his newest home away from home—if he had a home, which Fergus doubted—remembered seeing him again until six o'clock that night. Mrs. Horbal had died between one and three that afternoon. If it hadn't been much after one o'clock when she died, Boyd could have brought about her death. There would have been time for him to drive to Oldfield, push her down the cellar stairs, buy new clothes when he got back to Ridgeway, and be in his hotel room by six o'clock. Not a surplus of time, perhaps, but enough.

Fergus shook his head over this line of thought. For all he knew, Boyd, if asked, could account for every minute of last Wednesday afternoon. No fact or witness pointed to his presence in Oldfield. The doctor and state police officer on the scene found nothing to indicate that Mrs. Horbal's death wasn't an accident. Fergus had nothing, either, except his deep hostility toward the other man, based on what he had been to Andrea in the past and what he was doing to her in the present. But blackmail and murder, Fergus reminded himself, were not automatically related.

Nevertheless, he wished he had the authority to call Seymour Boyd to account for every minute of last Wednesday afternoon.

The rally in Eastham was scheduled for eight o'clock that night. Andrea and her father wound up a series of coffee hours in the vicinity at six and went to a nearby inn for dinner. When they were settled at a table, Andrew Langdon remarked that he was pleased with the turnout at the coffee hours, the variety of questions put to him, and the warmth of his reception wherever he went.

"Of course most of the people we met were dedicated Republicans, anyway," Andrea cautioned him. "It's too bad there aren't more independent voters at these affairs."

She had been reading Fergus every day on the election picture. More than once he had questioned the voting trend in Republican Ridgeway County this year. Even with an outstanding candidate like Andrew Langdon running in it, Fergus had found signs that it, too, might fall into the Democratic column.

When she mentioned this to her father, he smiled and said, "I can't afford to pay attention to MacDonald, no matter how well I think he knows his stuff. I've just got to keep plugging day in and day out. It's all I can do, all any man could do."

Andrea said lightly, "Well, one thing we don't have to do is order coffee with this meal. By the time November 4 comes around I doubt if I'll ever want to see another cup of coffee for the rest of my life."

Andrew Langdon laughed in agreement. "We'll

order tea tonight."

A moment later he eyed her with veiled concern. She said she'd got over her cold and felt fine but he thought she was too pale and had a fine-drawn look. The campaign was tiring, of course. They'd have to take a trip somewhere after it was over. In the meantime, he'd try not to rely so much on her, his lovely daughter who had been making friends for him all over the Sixth District since the campaign began.

He looked at her again. It was selfish of him to find so much enjoyment in her company. She should have married long ago and been devoting herself to her husband instead of her father. He ought to do something about it . . . but what? There'd been prospects enough; she had accepted none of them. He couldn't push her into a marriage she didn't want. In fact, he'd had to be on his guard against suitors who might be more interested in what she would inherit than in Andrea herself. He'd weeded out some and lent what encouragement he could to the desirables. But here was Andrea, going on twenty-eight and still single. Was it his fault, a question of his having turned to her too much since his retirement?

No, he thought, that couldn't be the answer. Andrea had been twenty-four, already moving past the average age for marriage, when he retired. Before that he had been too much occupied with business to foster interdependency between them. And yet Andrea hadn't married then and gave no sign of marrying now.

If he was elected to Congress, though, they'd have a change of scene. He'd rent a house in Georgetown, get her into the Washington social whirl, and hope that something would come of it.

He wanted her to marry. When his time came to die he didn't want her left alone without husband or children.

Children, he thought, smiling at her in a rush of sentiment. His grandchildren. How he would enjoy them. One of these days he would point it out to Andrea that it was every father's right to become a grandfather and spend his old age spoiling his grandchildren . . .

Andrea spoke of something else Fergus had written. The softness that came into her voice when she mentioned his name suddenly caught Andrew Langdon's attention. Well, he thought with an inward smile. Well . . .

He felt pleased. The more he saw of Fergus during the campaign the more he liked him. Here he was, worrying about Andrea's unmarried state, making plans to do something about it and all the while, it seemed, she might make her own plans in the matter.

Fergus's probable lack of money beyond what he earned and saved was of no great concern to Andrew Langdon who had so much of it himself. The only way in which it would really concern him would be if there was the least possibility that Fergus had his eye on what Andrea would one day inherit.

Fergus, Andrew Langdon thought — and he considered himself a good judge of men—wasn't that sort.

The next moment he laughed at himself. He was building a lot on a note in Andrea's voice.

He had better mind his own business for the present.

He drank his tea. Andrea drank hers. They talked about the speech he would make tonight. Today, not yet over, had consisted of one long effort to behave normally. Successful, she thought; no one, including her father, could guess at her true feelings.

Fergus was the exception. He knew too much of what was going on in her life to be deceived by surface composure. He arrived at Eastham Grange Hall where the rally was being held just as Andrew Langdon began his talk on problems in the district requiring federal aid.

Fergus heard little of what he said. Most of his attention was on Andrea, seated near her father. Her smile scarcely lifted the shadow on her face and didn't reach at all the somberness in her eyes.

When the speechmaking was over, coffee and sandwiches were served. The younger people in the audience sought out Andrea. She tried to be friendly but her thoughts were far away and pretense soon wore thin. Fergus waited for the right moment and then cut her out of the group.

He found a corner where they could sit down by themselves and said, "Just sit back and relax, Andrea. I think that's what you need."

She gave him a quick glance and looked away.

"I'm fine," she said. "It's been a long day, that's all."

"No, it isn't all." He spoke with quiet firmness. "Why try to convince me this is the best of all possible worlds when I know you've got a problem with Boyd? I shouldn't bring it up here but I've been trying to see you for days and you've been avoiding me. I could help you if you'd let me. May I see you sometime tomorrow?"

Her eyes were lowered, the lashes a dark curve above the delicate modeling of her cheekbones. Stark misery slipped through her guard when she finally looked at him. She said, "There's nothing, Fergus—"

"Just the same, may I see you tomorrow?"

"I'm sorry, but I'm afraid I can't manage it tomorrow. I'll be gone all day with my father. How did you like his speech tonight?"

He laid his hand over hers briefly. "Andrea, please."

Before she had to find an answer the town committee chairman came up with another man in tow. "Miss Langdon, here's a gentleman who'd like to meet you . . ."

After that it was no use. Other people joined them. Fergus said good night to her, talked for a few minutes with Andrew Langdon, and left. He didn't know what approach to try next with Andrea. He had known her only a few weeks. If he chose to fall in love with her—chose?—he'd had no choice, had he, from the moment he saw her on *Program Personality?*—but whether of his own choosing or not, loving her, wanting to help her had given him no rights at all. Andrea had made this plain enough. She had twice rejected his offer of help.

It was a hard fact to accept. He wouldn't accept it. Andrea's withdrawal into a shell he could not penetrate had nothing to do with him personally; it had to do with Seymour Boyd and all that he stood for. It was up to Fergus to get rid of him. Until he did, he had no chance of persuading her that the past, a thing without remedy, need not blight the future for them. It occurred to him suddenly that the Langdon money no longer constituted a barrier in his thoughts of Andrea. Getting rid of Seymour Boyd had become infinitely more important.

Chapter Eighteen

Andrea's mail the next morning did not include the check from the Littleton bank. She spent the day with her father on a tour of industrial areas of the Sixth District, talking and shaking hands with men at their machines and benches, in cafeterias and at factory gates.

Fergus didn't call her. She should have been relieved that he had finally taken no for an answer; but so inconsistent a thing was her heart, she discovered, that his defection lay like a stone on it.

Thursday morning's mail brought the check from the Littleton bank. Andrea waited until her father left for Republican headquarters and then set out for her bank in Ridgeway with the check. On the way she thought about getting it cashed. It was going to be an awkward procedure. If she walked into her bank and asked for fifty thousand dollars in cash, every eyebrow in the place would be raised. Then, too, how bulky would the money be in twenties and fifties? She was carrying a big handbag but she should have brought along a brief case. She'd have to buy one.

Her nerve failed her when she reached the bank. She deposited the check from Littleton but the one she made out to cash was for only ten thousand. Then, when she took it to a teller's station, her cheeks grew hot with the irrational conviction that he must know why she needed that much cash. She couldn't bring herself to ask for twenties and let him count out half in hundreds, half in fifties. He put them in an envelope, a wad so thick that doubled over it bulged out her handbag.

But that was only the beginning. She bought a brief case, went on to a bank where she was known slightly, and wrote another check for ten thousand, again accepting the money in fifties and hundreds.

At the third bank she went to she wasn't known at all and had to establish her identity and wait for verification of the check before she could cash it. She felt as if all eyes were on her while she waited. She would have to cash smaller checks hereafter even if it meant going to every bank in Ridgeway.

By two o'clock that afternoon Andrea had cashed checks for the full amount although very little of it was in twenties. By three, going from teller to teller in downtown banks, she had ten thousand dollars in twenties and thirty thousand in fifties. Seymour would have to accept the remaining ten thousand in hundreds; she would not, she told herself, go through again tomorrow morning what she had gone through today.

She went home with the brief case. Before she

left the house to go to a dinner party that night, she locked it up in a chest in her room. She had no other place to keep it; she could hardly ask her father to put it in the safe downstairs.

Early that evening Fergus found time to drop in on Condon at the Wilton. The security officer had a person-to-person phone call to report on. It had come in an hour ago through an operator in Hotchkissville. The conversation was brief. The man who called said he had got home from work with something on his mind he wanted to talk over. Boyd said all right, he'd be out to see him that evening, and hung up. Twenty minutes ago he'd left the hotel and driven off in his car.

Yesterday, Condon continued, when his bill for the week was presented to him, he'd paid it promptly in cash. Last night he'd got pretty drunk, not falling down drunk but fairly close to it, in the bar. The bartender said he tried to pick a fight with another patron who left when the bartender started to intervene. After that Seymour quieted down for a little while. Then he began to ramble on in the bartender's ear about the tough breaks he'd had all his life, people double-crossing him, pulling the rug out from under him every time it looked as if things might go his way. But now, he said, the picture was changed. He had it made from here on in; when he left this graveyard town he'd have the world by the tail.

Just before closing time he got very loud again. The bartender tried to ease him out but he refused to budge. He was a big shot now, he said, and no one was going to push him around any more. It was so near closing time that the bartender didn't make an issue of it but confined himself to turning a deaf ear when Seymour demanded another. The bar closed and Seymour left without assistance. And if he never came back, the bartender said, it would suit him fine; he'd seen all kinds but this character, quarrelsome and boastful by turns, not even a mother could love.

"So," Condon concluded, "it looks as if he's got it set up, whatever it is."

"Uh-huh," Fergus said.

"When you going to give me the lowdown on this deal?"

"As soon as I know what it is myself." Fergus tried to sound convincing but Condon's disgruntled look announced his disbelief. He needed placating. A bottle of Canadian Club had a very placating effect on him, Fergus had learned in the past. But this time a more generous gesture was in order. On the way back to his office Fergus stopped at a liquor store and ordered a case of Canadian Club to be delivered immediately to the security officer.

He had a story to finish for tomorrow's paper. First he phoned Andrea. The maid said she'd gone out for the evening and asked if there was a message.

"No message." As Fergus hung up, from sheer frustration he gave passing thought to pulling the phone out of the wall. Instead he sat glumly at his desk, wondering where Andrea was tonight, how much of a pay-off she had to make, and when she was going to make it. Then he wondered what was going on at that very moment between Seymour and Walt Horbal. It must be something important to Horbal. He had kept in the background so far. But now he had initiated a move himself through his phone call.

Seymour was seething as he set out for Oldfield. Walt's call to the hotel had placed on record a link between them, and the demanding tone he had taken had done nothing to mend matters. Seymour was sick of Walt; sick of the long drive to Oldfield; sick of the feeling that he was running a gauntlet every time he drove through the center, crouched over the wheel in the hope that Madame Defarge in her store window wouldn't see him; sick of creeping in and out of the gravel road, on the alert for prying eyes; and above all, sick of keeping up a show of friendliness with a piece of trash like Walt Horbal.

During the drive his fit of temper abated. By tomorrow night at this time it would be all over. He'd have seen the last of Horbal—until he needed him again—and he'd be on his way to New York, his starting point. He'd check into a good hotel with a bottle of good bourbon, room service jumping at his beck and call, and—well, hell, how long had it been since he'd had a woman?

The bourbon came first, of course; but there were moments when he thought about women and felt uneasy over the way his interest in them decreased year by year. His lack of money must be to blame, he reflected. Once he had plenty of it; what the hell, he'd hit his stride, get all the old fire back

When Walt opened the front door to admit him,

Seymour found himself suddenly reluctant to go into the house. He hadn't been inside it since he killed Effie a week ago yesterday and didn't want to go into it now. He hesitated on the threshold until Walt rumbled, "What the hell's eatin' you? You going to stand on the doorstep all night?" Then, conquering his reluctance, he went in.

They sat down in the sitting room where Effie had precipitated the scene that ended in her death. It had been all her own fault, Seymour reminded himself, selecting a chair out of direct range of the one Effie had occupied last week. If she hadn't threatened him with the police she'd be sitting in that chair tonight.

"Well, what's on your mind?" he inquired of Walt and added, "I could do with a drink."

"Let's talk business first and have a drink afterwards." Walt's tone was surly. He sat on a straight chair, his thick hands planted on his knees. "I think we're missing the boat in this deal, letting Miss Lambert—Langdon off the hook so easy. Twenty thousand is peanuts to her. Down the street from the mill in Hotchkissville there's a big piece of land for sale and a fellow that works with me said today he heard Grocery Mart's bought it and they're going to build a supermarket there. Jesus, when you think of the money her old man's got!"

They had gone into this Monday while Fergus watched from the underbrush and wondered what they were talking about. Seymour had told Walt then that he'd asked Andrea for twenty thousand. Walt had argued that it wasn't enough and apparently had been brooding over it ever since. What he'd heard today about a Grocery Mart in Hotch-kissville had been all that was needed to bring his grievance to a head.

"You're too goddamn chicken, that's what's the matter with you," he said. "You could of put the bite on her for two or three times that much. We got her over a barrel. What could she do but pay?"

Seymour, with fifty thousand coming in tomorrow, could afford to remain calm. He replied with only a trace of arrogance, "As I pointed out to you the other day, Mr. Horbal, it's not Miss Langdon who controls the purse strings, it's her father. I went into her own resources with her. Twenty thousand is the limit she can raise right now, and I have no desire to drive her to the wall on it. After all, this is only the first time we expect to carry the pitcher to the well, you know. If we keep our demands within reason, she's much more apt to meet them." He made a negligent gesture. "But why go into all that again? It seems to me we covered it quite thoroughly the other day."

Walt eyed him suspiciously. His dislike of Seymour, nurtured from their first meeting, bordered on hatred. If there was one type he couldn't stand, he told himself, it was a smooth-talking, educated bastard like this guy, putting on airs, acting like he was better than Walt. And to hear him talk about the pitcher and the well you'd think they were going to get away with putting the bite on Miss Langdon every time they felt like it. He wanted no part of that kind of a deal and no part of Seymour ever again. Give him one good cut and he'd head back to Nevada and call it quits. What they were working on wasn't the gold mine it was supposed to be. It was blackmail that could blow up in their faces any time at all.

He said sourly, "I don't like the way you got it set up. I got different ideas. I'm ready to sell this place for anything it will bring and clear out of here. I'm going back to Las Vegas. I got my eye on a widow out there with a nice little restaurant business. She's got a lot of get-up-and-go to her. I figure we can team up and make out fine. All I want is a damn good stake to take out there with me so she won't think I'm after what she's got."

Seymour studied him. Was there actually a widow in Las Vegas or anywhere else who would have the man? He looked like a toad squatting on the chair, hamlike hands on his knees, open shirt showing a mat of hair on his chest, belly hanging out over the waistband of his trousers. Once there had been a prostitute in Baltimore who had supported Seymour for months and sometimes when she was drunk shook her head at him and mumbled, "For every old shoe there's an old stocking." He remembered this without his usual resentment of it as he looked at Walt Horbal. Perhaps it applied to him. Perhaps there was a widow in Las Vegas—or somewhere on the face of the earth—who would have him.

Seymour said, with condescension breaking through the elaborately patient note in his voice, "I have no reason to disbelieve Miss Langdon when she says twenty thousand is all she can possibly raise right now." (He prided himself on referring to Andrea as Miss Langdon in front of Walt. Bad luck

218

had brought him low, but not so low that he didn't try at times to remember he had been brought up a gentleman, whereas Walt Horbal had never been anything more than the lout he was today.)

"But it's only ten thousand apiece," Walt protested. "Not a drop in the bucket to her. She's playing you for a sucker."

"Nobody plays me for a sucker," Seymour replied sharply. "Ever."

Walt glowered at him. "There's always a first time."

Seymour started to glower back but checked himself. Why should he let this stupid lout get his goat? After all, he was the one who was being played for a sucker, taking Seymour's word for it that all Andrea could pay was twenty thousand. The only thing that was really irritating about his attitude was his assumption that they should go halves on the money when none of the risk or trouble had fallen on him.

"Look," he began, and in spite of the fact that he would need Walt in the future and should stay on good terms with him, Seymour couldn't quite keep the note of a pedagogue dealing with a backward pupil out of his voice, "people with money don't have it where they can lay their hands on it overnight. It's tied up in real estate or stocks and bonds or whatever. That's Miss Langdon's difficulty. She'd have to go through her father to raise more than twenty thousand. When she explained her position to me, I could see what she meant; and the last thing we want is for her father to get wind of it. So isn't it better to take twenty thousand now and come back for another twenty thousand later? And here's another point to consider: Langdon won't live forever and his daughter's his only heir. After he's dead is the time we really move in on her. Meanwhile, let's settle for what we can get as we go along."

"I still say get more now and let the future take care of itself," Walt grumbled. But Seymour noticed that he spoke with less conviction. Brains over brawn, of course. This lout could be led around by the nose.

The open hostility between them diminished a little. Seymour painted a rosy picture of their prospects and discussed how they could best keep in touch with each other for future collaboration after they went their separate ways the day after tomorrow.

He had lied to Walt about the pay-off date, suspecting that if he said it was tomorrow Walt, not trusting him an inch, would show up bright and early in Ridgeway and follow him to the rendezvous with Andrea. He had no intention of permitting that.

Presently Walt gave him a drink. Before Seymour left, they were on, what were for them, fairly good terms.

But when Walt was alone again in the house, moving restlessly from room to room, noting without interest the signs of dust and disorder beginning to accumulate with Effie eight days dead, all his previous suspicion and resentment of Seymour returned full force. He was a fool, he told himself gloomily, letting Boyd run the whole show, taking his word for everything. He was entitled to some say in this affair, wasn't he? If he didn't look after his own interests, who would? Not Boyd, not that slippery bastard, no sir, not by a damned sight . . .

Chapter Nineteen

Fergus was out of bed early the next morning. He hadn't slept well. He had Andrea on his mind.

He made himself breakfast at his apartment, stacked the dishes in the sink with yesterday morning's, and went to Ridgeway police headquarters. The desk sergeant informed him that Lieutenant Brandon was in and let Fergus make his own way through the corridors to the detective bureau.

Fergus had known the lieutenant since his police-reporter days when Brandon was a detective, third grade. They had both moved up in their respective fields since that time and along the way had kept up an intermittent friendship. Brandon, Fergus felt, could be trusted with whatever it was necessary to tell him of the story and was well qualified to give advice and assistance.

They shook hands and sat down in the lieutenant's office. Fergus asked how Mrs. Brandon and the children were and talked of this or that for a few minutes. Then, getting out cigarettes, he said,

"Rick, I've got a problem about blackmail. It's not mine actually but I'm trying to take it over — without, I might add, the consent or cooperation of the victim."

"Well," Brandon said. "Well . . ." He looked mildly taken aback. He was a man intelligent above the average, several years older than Fergus, his fortieth birthday on the horizon, his hair gray at the temples, his eyes contemplative and faintly weary from almost two decades of looking upon humanity's sin and folly and woe passing in review before him.

"Sounds very officious of me, doesn't it?" Fergus said.

"Well, yes, now that you mention it. A lady, I suppose?"

Now it was Fergus who looked taken aback. Brandon smiled. "Naturally," he said. "Did you check your sword and plumes at the door?" His smile faded. "What's it all about?"

Fergus told him, his only omission from the story the reason why Andrea was vulnerable to blackmail, but everything he knew about Seymour brought in, his sudden affluence, his trips to Oldfield, Effie Horbal's death, the money given Walt, Seymour's drunken boasts in the hotel bar about having it made from now on.

"With a setup like that," he said at the end, "it can't be anything but blackmail."

The lieutenant nodded, steepled his fingers and studied the effect. He said, "But what can I do, Fergus, if Miss Langdon won't move against this man, won't come to the police and sign a com-

223

plaint? Have you tried to get her to? What does she say?"

Fergus had to confess that Andrea wouldn't discuss the matter with him, wouldn't even admit there was anything to discuss. "She doesn't dare to, Rick," he added for the benefit of Brandon's raised eyebrows. "She's in a terrible spot right now with her father running for Congress."

"This unmentioned blot on her past—do you know what it is yourself?"

"Yes. Not because she told me but because I made it my business to find out."

"Would she be liable to arrest if it came out?"

"Good lord, no!" Fergus was emphatic in denial. Then he said, "It's just one of those things. Something that happened years ago. A tragedy."

"They always are." The lieutenant's eyes were a shade wearier as they rested on Fergus. "But with nothing to work on, what can I do about it?"

Fergus explained what he had in mind. He wanted Brandon to accompany him when he went to see Seymour to tell him he knew what he was up to and that he wasn't going to be allowed to get away with it.

The lieutenant frowned in disapproval. "I don't like making empty threats." He reached for a pencil and began to draw faces on a pad. "I don't like blackmailers either. The scum of the earth." He paused. "So what would we do if he laughed in our faces and told us he didn't know what we were talking about?"

"I'm hoping he wouldn't, not with you along. If he did—" Fergus's jaw tightened. "I guess what I

224

really want is a chance to beat the hell out of him."

"What good would that do Miss Langdon?"

"None. But it would do me a lot of good. Here's another thing, Rick: A man like Boyd probably has a record somewhere. Maybe it could be used to scare him off for good."

"Maybe." Brandon's tone was not without sympathy as he went on, "But is Miss Langdon going to thank you for this? If she prefers to pay rather than risk exposure it seems to me you're on delicate ground."

"I know." Fergus gave him a wry grin. "I don't expect her to thank me. But her life's plain hell right now. She needs help whether she wants it or not." His face took on stubbornness. "I'm going to try to give it to her. She has nothing to lose by it. Boyd won't talk while there's profit in keeping what he knows about her to himself. And if he can't be scared off, at least he'll know a police officer and a newspaperman are on to him."

"I could get his prints. Be a break if he was wanted somewhere."

Fergus brightened, then drew his black brows together and shook his head. "Too good to be true."

After a moment's silence Brandon said, "Of course I couldn't touch this thing officially the way it stands now. But I suppose if I go to see Boyd with you when I'm off duty and you introduce me as a police lieutenant, it might do some good."

They talked it over. Fergus said he wouldn't be able to reach Condon this early in the day but would check with him on Seymour's whereabouts later on before the lieutenant went off duty at four o'clock. If Seymour was then available, they would go straight to the hotel to see him.

When he left police headquarters Fergus felt that he had taken the best action open to him. He also felt uncomfortable over what Andrea's attitude would be if it became necessary to tell her what he had done. He had been, to say the least, presumptuous. He loved her. That was the only excuse he had.

At three o'clock that afternoon Andrea, the brief case in her hand, went into Smalley's Grill. Again Seymour was there ahead of her in the same rear booth and rose to greet her with his usual punctilious courtesy. The waitress appeared and went away when Andrea told her she wasn't going to order anything.

Seymour took the brief case from her and, although the restaurant was virtually deserted, shielded it with his body while he opened it.

His breath escaped in an involuntary whistle at the sight of the money, packets and packets of it, each with a rubber band around it. But his face darkened when he took one out. "This is in hundreds. I told you—"

"Yes, you told me. But ten thousand of it is in hundreds. The rest is in fifties and twenties. Did you ever stop to think how much was involved in getting fifty thousand dollars in smaller bills?"

"What do you mean? All you had to do was walk into your bank—"

"No," Andrea said, "that wasn't all I had to do. It would have caused talk that might have got back

226

to my father. It's his bank, too. I went all over Ridgeway, Seymour. It took most of yesterday. But the hundreds are not marked bills. Neither are the fifties or twenties. You'll be able to spend them as freely as you please."

Her tone was dry. For the first time since he had come back into her life, and only for the moment, she felt in command of the situation. She stood up to leave and looked at him, her gentle blue eyes icy with contempt. "If you can bear to wait that long you'd better take the money back to your room to count it. Every dollar is there of the money you're blackmailing out of me for a thing you share the guilt of as much as I. But I can't believe that even a person as horrible as you will find much pleasure in spending it."

He was on his feet as soon as she, his eyes slits of anger. "You're a little late in finding me horrible, aren't you?" he taunted her. "Ten years ago, for instance, if I'd just waved a wedding ring at you —"

Andrea held his glance for a moment and then without a word turned and walked away.

He called after her, "I won't say good-by, Andrea. Just au revoir."

The waitress, idling near the cash register, looked at her with open curiosity. Andrea, her head high, walked out of the restaurant.

Seymour didn't move until she was gone. Then he beckoned for his check, left no tip because he thought he detected a glint of amusement in the waitress's eye — that would teach her not to laugh at him over what she thought was a lovers' quarrel in which he'd got the worst of it — and with the brief case held tight under his arm went back to the Wilton.

He spread the money out on his bed and counted it, not because he felt it was necessary—Andrea knew better than to shortchange him—but just for the pleasure of it, the feel of the crisp bills, the marvelous, unaccustomed feel of them, twelve hundred of them altogether, passport to a brand new world.

While he gloated over the green counterpane they made on the bed, one corner of his mind dwelt on Walt Horbal. God, he groaned to himself presently, how he hated to hand over one fifth of this wonderful stuff to a lout who had done nothing, not one solitary thing, to earn it.

What if he just cleared out with the whole fifty thousand? As far as the lout knew, he wasn't supposed to collect it until tomorrow. He'd have a twenty-four-hour start. He could be in Miami, Havana, Jamaica, any number of places by the time Horbal got it through his thick skull that he'd been gypped.

This was an idea Seymour had been toying with for days. Two factors restrained him from carrying it out. Walt, seeking revenge and blind to the consequences to himself, might go to the police with the story; although there was little the police could do about it without confirmation from Andrea, still it would mean that he could never try to collect from her again. And even if Walt had sense enough not to go to the police, he couldn't be approached at a future time for further collaboration on blackmail.

Seymour gave a sigh of resignation. In the long run, it was to his better advantage to pay the lout his alleged half. How long would it take him to go through it? Well, that depended to some extent on the widow in Las Vegas. But in two years' time Horbal ought to be more than ready to try again. It would be just the right time, too. If Langdon got elected, he'd be running for a second term in another two years and Andrea would be more anxious than ever to avoid exposure.

Yes, he'd have to pay Horbal.

He began to sort the bills. Twenty thousand in fifties and twenties went back into the brief case. The hundreds and as many fifties as would fit went into the money belt he had bought that morning. The rest of the fifties went into an envelope in his suitcase.

His clothes were already packed. He called the desk and asked to have his bill made out and a bellhop sent up.

There was time for a drink while he waited. But when he picked up his only bottle he was chagrined to find it empty. He'd had too much on his mind today to buy a fresh supply.

Ten minutes later, his hotel bill paid, his suitcase locked in the trunk of the car, the brief case on the seat beside him, the money belt tight around his waist, Seymour was ready to start for Oldfield. The bellboy, rendered obsequious in farewell by a five-dollar tip, closed the door after him. Seymour, on top of the world, drove out of the parking lot.

It was twenty minutes of four. Two hours to Oldfield, half an hour with Horbal, and he'd be on his way with forty thousand dollars in his pocket. Not bad, he thought jubilantly, for a man who'd been down and out less than a month ago. Not bad at all.

The late afternoon traffic was heavy. Making his way through it was slow work. Thirsty work, too. On the outskirts of Ridgeway a bar loomed invitingly. Seymour slowed down and stopped. He might as well have a quick one to make up for the empty bottle in his room.

Chapter Twenty

At quarter of four that afternoon Condon, after two attempts, finally located Fergus at the office of the *Post,* in conference with the Sunday magazine editor, and told him Seymour had checked out a few minutes ago. "Throwing money around, too," he added. "Five-dollar tips all over the place."

"Oh," Fergus said slowly. "Well, thanks a lot for letting me know."

He hung up, excused himself to the Sunday magazine editor, and hurried back to his desk. He called Andrea first. The maid said she was lying down and could not be disturbed. That was all right with Fergus. He would go to see her.

He called Brandon at police headquarters and when he had him on the line said, "Look, Rick, I think the pay-off's been made and I'm going right out to see the lady and find out for sure. If I'm right, our man must be on his way to Oldfield now to divide the profits, so we'll have to move fast. We can take a short cut, though, a country road this side of High Point. It's near a little bridge with a gas station on the corner. Do you know the one I mean?"

"Yes, I guess I do."

"You'll be off duty in a few minutes. Will you meet me there?"

"Okay," the lieutenant said. "I'll be there — for what it's worth, with both hands tied behind my back and out of my jurisdiction, too."

His tone was weighted with misgivings. But he would be on hand to do what he could.

Andrea had gone straight home when she left Seymour. Exhausted, she asked for nothing except to lie on the chaise longue in her room with her eyes closed and no need to move or speak.

At twenty minutes past four Hilda knocked on the door and said apologetically, "Mr. MacDonald is here, Miss Langdon. I told him you couldn't be disturbed but he said to tell you it's very important for him to see you right away."

"Thank you, Hilda. Tell him I'll be right down."

Fergus was here. A small ray of brightness flickered through the dead pall of Andrea's mood. She went to her dressing table, smoothed her hair, and put on lipstick. It was a soft shade but even so, her face was so pale, her fair skin almost transparent in its pallor, that the lipstick made too bright a contrast and she wiped most of it off. Then she shook out the full skirt of her dress and went downstairs.

Fergus was waiting in the living room. He hadn't removed his topcoat although he had unbuttoned it and had his hands shoved in the pockets. He stood near a window and turned toward her as she came into the room. "Hello, Andrea," he said.

"Hello, Fergus."

There was constraint between them. "Won't you sit down?" she said.

"I'm afraid there isn't time." His dark eyes searched her face. "You paid off Boyd today, didn't you?"

"Fergus, please—"

"Yes, I know it's none of my business but I'm not staying out of it. And I haven't time to be diplomatic . . ." Gentleness came into his voice. "I know the whole story, Andrea." He reached for her hands and wouldn't release them when she tried to pull free. "I know, I tell you."

She stood still. "No."

"Yes. Little Sir 915, all of it."

He thought she would collapse at his feet and held her with both arms around her.

Sobs shook her. "I can't bear it," she said over and over. "I can't, I can't—"

"It's going to be all right, darling." He stroked her hair, trying to soothe her. "Everything will be all right."

"Seymour told you. I gave him the money but still he told you."

"Oh no!" Fergus was shocked. "Do you think I'd listen to anything he tried to tell me about you? I found it out for myself."

"After all these years of hiding it," she sobbed. "The lies I've told—the way I've tried to pretend I was like other girls—you don't know—but oh, he was so sweet. Years and years— You don't know how sweet he was." In broken gasps she sobbed on

Fergus's shoulder. "If only just once I could have heard him call me 'mommy'! If only just once—"

"Darling," Fergus said. "Darling, we'll talk it all over later but now I've got to go. I've got to do something about Boyd." He led her to the sofa. "I'm crazy about you," he said tenderly. "You know that, don't you?" His hand cupped her chin and lifted up her head. He kissed her lips. "I'll be back as fast as I can. I may not get your money back but I'm going to Oldfield now and make sure neither of that pair ever comes near you again."

Alarm flashed across her face. "You can't do anything with Seymour. If you try, he'll tell people about Greg."

"No he won't. I'll see to that. Fergus's face turned grim. "How much did you pay him?"

"Fifty thousand dollars."

"God!"

"Let it go," she said. "I don't care about the money. Just let it go."

"No. If he gets away with it this time he'll be back for more."

She wasn't listening. "He had such a shy little smile," she said. "He was so sweet. I loved him so much. But when I knew he was dead I didn't claim his body. I let him be called an unidentified victim. I let him be buried in an anonymous grave. It was as if he was a homeless stray kitten. Then when I saw the pictures of him in the *Post*—" She couldn't go on. She buried her face in her hands.

Fergus bent over her. "Andrea, it's past. But if it would help you to talk about it at last, that's what I want you to do as soon as there's time. Right now,

234

though, I've got to leave." He touched her hair in a caress. "You gave Boyd the money today?"

"Yes, this afternoon."

"Well, I'd better get moving." He took her hands from her face and kissed her. "Go back up to your room, darling; have a good cry and get it all out of your system. But remember one thing: After all this time you're not alone with it any more; you're never going to be alone with it again."

He started for the door. She said, "Oh, Fergus, you mustn't go. What can you do against two of them, two evil men? They might do something to you!"

Her alarm was for him now. He looked back and said, "I have an old and trustworthy friend, a police lieutenant, who's meeting me, Andrea. I haven't told him the whole story, of course. Just enough so that between us we can handle that pair." He smiled at her reassuringly. "There's nothing to worry about. That's a promise."

He was gone. The front door closed behind him before Andrea could utter another protest. She ran to the door but he was already in his car, racing down the driveway. She watched until he was out of sight. Her moment of alarm was suddenly supplanted by the deep conviction that Fergus, with his quiet self-assurance, could take care of himself and deal with Seymour, too, in such a fashion that he would never dare to come back again. She had seen the last of him.

She went upstairs to her room but she didn't cry when she reached it. She had no tears to shed just now. She went into the bathroom and bathed her

235

eyes and tidied her hair. Her telephone rang. It was a person-to-person call from Walt Horbal, switched over to her from the push-button system downstairs.

He said, "This is Walt Horbal, Miss Langdon."

"Yes?"

"I'm going back to Nevada."

"Are you?"

"Yeah. But this thing you've got fixed up with our friend in Ridgeway, I don't like it much. I figure if I had more of a stake I'd stay out there and never come back."

"That's something you should take up with your partner. As I understand it, he's to take care of you out of the fifty thousand and I—"

A strangled exclamation at the other end of the line cut her short. Then Walt spluttered. "Fifty— did you say—fifty thousand?"

"Yes."

"Well, I'll be—" He slammed down the receiver so hard that it jarred Andrea's eardrum. She hung up slowly herself with a worried frown. She tried to sort out the conversation. Apparently Seymour had lied to Walt Horbal about how much money she had given him. She had no way to let Fergus know about this or if it should enter into his approach to the pair.

She stood up from the telephone and walked back and forth around the room. The importance of the call began to lessen in her mind. It didn't matter so much, after all, she thought. Fergus and his police-lieutenant friend would surely be equal to coping with any change that came from it.

She sat down by a window and looked out with unseeing eyes. The next few hours until Fergus returned would be long and hard to live through. But underneath suspense there was room for other feelings, the first faint thawing of the spirit, frozen so long ago into its pattern of guilt and sorrow and shame. Fergus knew the truth about her. He accepted it. He had called her "darling." He had said, "I'm crazy about you. You know that, don't you?" He had kissed her. He had said, "After all this time you're not alone with it any more; you're never going to be alone with it again."

He had set her free to welcome and return his love.

Chapter Twenty-one

Seymour's quick one in the bar became two and then three. He got into conversation with a salesman for an investment firm in Ridgeway and talked expansively about the investments he meant to make in the near future out of an inheritance from an uncle whose favorite nephew he had been. His uncle's death from a heart attack, details of his funeral, and the grief Seymour felt were poured out while the salesman, scenting a prospect, made appropriate comment. This took them through the drink the salesman insisted on buying. While they had another—Seymour's treat—chemicals, electronics, and missiles were discussed, Seymour confiding that most of his holdings were in conservative blue chips and that it was time they underwent a thorough study with an eye to changes that might lead to greater growth potential.

The gleam in the salesman's eye reflected the visions of fat commissions that danced in his head. Eventually he suggested looking over a list of Seymour's holdings and pinned him down to an appointment the following Monday morning at eleven o'clock.

Three quarters of an hour had elapsed since Seymour had gone into the bar. He exclaimed over the time—he'd be late for an important business meeting—shook hands with the salesman, assuring him he'd see him Monday at eleven, and left.

The salesman felt pleased with himself. Monday's appointment could be dangled in front of his wife when she started in on him the minute he got into the house about hanging around in bars. You never knew who you'd meet, he'd tell her. Look at the money I could make from this appointment Monday. And how'd I get it? From hanging around in a bar.

The salesman had been hanging around in it too long. His judgment was the worse for it.

With daylight-saving time still in effect, night hadn't quite fallen at quarter of seven when Seymour arrived at Walt Horbal's. Lights shone from the house. Walt was home. Seymour, with thoughts of leaving the money somewhere on the premises, would just as soon have found him absent. He went up to the front door and reached for the bell.

Before he could ring it, the door opened and Walt, a heavy black bulk against the light behind him, said, "Come in."

He wore a suit coat, Seymour noticed, when they faced each other in the sitting room, the first time he had seen him in anything but his shirtsleeves. It didn't add a formal note to his appearance, though, not with a stubble of beard adorning his chin and work pants and a work shirt, open at the neck, completing his costume. His right hand was in the coat pocket. It sagged a little.

It was irrelevant, this attention to the way Walt was dressed, but still Seymour noticed it before his glance went to Walt's face.

It wore a scowl. The eyes bored into him. "Day early, aren't you?" His murderous mood only slightly controlled, Walt waited to hear what Seymour was going to say.

Seymour smiled cheerfully. He was in a fine mood, not in the least drunk, just mellow from the combination of drinks and dreams of his brand-new world to come. "Payday was today instead of tomorrow," he announced. "Y'know, I think Miss Langdon wanted to get me the hell out of Ridgeway as fast as she could—can't imagine why, can you?—because she phoned this morning that she had the money ready. I, of course, raised no objections to collecting it today. So here I am, sir, ready to split the take, shake hands, and say good-by until the next time."

"You didn't call me you were coming." Walt's voice was hoarse and he breathed noisily through his mouth, but Seymour, wrapped in his dreams, paid no attention. "I couldn't wait that long to get out of Ridgeway," he said. "Like a homing pigeon I winged my way here with the spoils of war—a very small war at that—"

He rambled on, his fox's grin wide and happy with a good will that embraced even Walt at the moment. He set the brief case on a table and, after a glance at the windows to make sure the shades

240

were drawn, opened it.

Walt cut in on his ramblings. "What if I hadn't been home?"

The red eyebrows rose in patient acceptance of stupidity. "Elementary, my dear Watson, elementary. If you hadn't been home I'd have nosed about until I found a safe hiding place for your share and later tonight phoned you from somewhere along the road to tell you where to conduct your treasure hunt."

Seymour's hands were busy as he talked, removing packets of money from the brief case. When he had them all laid out, they covered the surface of the round, old-fashioned table.

Walt drew closer, his jaw hanging open, a mesmerized glaze coming over his eyes as they fastened on the money. Seymour stood and looked at it, too, like a proud new father viewing his first-born child. In the sudden silence Walt's breathing rasped through the room. "How much does it come to?" he asked.

As he drew closer, Seymour caught the smell of sweat from him, wrinkled his nose fastidiously, and moved back a step. Walt's menacing look was lost on Seymour, whose attention was fastened on the money. "What a foolish question," he said with easy condescension. "I told you I'd get twenty thousand and that's what I got. We might as well—"

"Goddamn you to hell for a lying son of a bitch!" With clubbed fist, Walt knocked him across the room.

Seymour crashed against the wall, bounced off

241

it, and slid to the floor. Shaking his head groggily, he lay there until Walt, a raging bull, started for him again. Just in time he rolled out of the way. He staggered to his feet, got behind the table, and began to move around it, edging toward the door.

Walt had no use for such finesse. One shove of his powerful arms sent the table over, money flying in all directions.

Seymour was no more of a match for Walt than Effie had been for him. He went down with Walt on top of him, astride of him, hammering him with his fists. Rockets of pain roared through Seymour's head. Blood gushed from his nose and broken teeth.

"You double-crossing bastard," Walt snarled. "I don't need a gun for you. By Christ, I don't want one. This is the way to do it."

Gun. The word penetrated the haze engulfing Seymour. Gun. The suit coat, never worn before. The hard object in the pocket cutting into his side.

The blows ceased abruptly; the crushing weight was removed. Walt had discovered the money belt. With a muttered ejaculation he tore it off him.

Seymour couldn't open one eye at all. He could open the other far enough to see the crouching figure swearing furiously over this proof positive of treachery and double-dealing.

With immense effort Seymour's hand inched its way to Walt's sagging right pocket.

"Jesus, look at it, look at it!" Walt shouted. "Hundred dollar bills—oh you dirty bastard, I'll kill you for this; I'll kill—"

The roar of the .38, deafening at this range, cut

off his voice and his life. Three times Seymour shot him.

Walt toppled forward from his crouch and fell sidewise on the floor.

Seymour sat up slowly and cried out with pain when he moved his head. It seemed an endless time before he was able to get up on his knees and then his feet. He clung to a chair for support and looked around dazedly. Money lay scattered everywhere, some of it under the bleeding body on the floor. Brief case—where was it? His half-open eye searched the room and located the brief case over by a window. Pick up the money. Would he be able to drive? He had to. Wash himself, find a drink—must be one in the house—get going. He had to get going. He couldn't lean on this chair all night . . .

Chapter Twenty-two

Lieutenant Brandon drove to Oldfield, Fergus leaving his car at the gas station where they met. They took the country road, the short cut, but they had a later start than Seymour. It was after seven o'clock when they turned off on the gravel road to Walt Horbal's. Night had almost fallen; only a faint glow of light lingered in the west.

After they passed the deserted house, Fergus said, "You'd better turn off your lights now, Rick."

They crept forward after that, the semidarkness less dense as their eyes grew accustomed to it.

Around the last bend before the farmhouse they saw its lights ahead. The lieutenant pulled over to the side of the road and shut off the motor. They went forward on foot, picking out the silhouette of Seymour's car in the driveway, with another car, presumably Walt Horbal's, in front of it.

There were lights in the front and rear of the

house. In the front the shades were drawn, with only an edging of light showing around them. When they were about three hundred feet away, Brandon called a halt. "Before we go up and ring the doorbell, let's try to see what's going on," he said. "I'll try the front windows; you try the back. But first take a good look at the car and make sure it's Boyd's. We don't want to—"

The sound of shots coming from inside the house, at that distance, sounded like firecrackers going off. But not to Brandon's trained ear. "My God, somebody's shooting off a gun in there," he said. He started forward at a cautious trot, throwing a command at Fergus over his shoulder to stay out of it; it was his job to handle this.

But Fergus was close behind him, following his example in taking advantage of every bit of cover that offered itself.

Screened by a tall shrub at the edge of the driveway, Brandon said in a fierce whisper, "Fergus, don't move another foot. I told you to stay out of it and I meant it. You haven't got a gun and I don't intend to have you gumming this thing up and maybe getting a bullet through you, too. Stay right where you are. That's an order."

Fergus gave a tense little laugh. "Okay," he said and, from the shadow of the shrub, watched the lieutenant dart across the driveway and melt into the wall of the house. Straining to see what he did next, Fergus caught a glimpse of him flat against the wall at the rear, ducking forward to look into the lighted kitchen. He lost him then until the light around the drawn shade in front picked him out briefly, moving out of range of the window. In another moment Fergus felt his scalp prickle with ancient fears as the sinister quiet was broken by Brandon who shouted, "Boyd! Horbal! I'm a police officer and I've got this place surrounded. Whichever one of you is still alive, drop that gun and come out with your hands up!"

In the sitting room Seymour labored over picking up the money and putting it in the brief case, each move exquisite torture for his battered body. When the shout came, it paralyzed him with shock.

He recovered mobility when Brandon shouted again. In the urgencies of the moment he forgot about his physical condition. He snatched up the gun and brief case and reached for the light switch. With the room plunged into darkness he paused to think. Was the place really surrounded? There was only one voice and it came from outside the sitting-room window; was he expected to break for the front door? His car was nearer the back door. He had to get to it. He wouldn't have a Chinaman's chance on foot in this lonely countryside.

When Brandon shouted his third warning, Seymour was scurrying through the kitchen on hands and knees, hugging the wall under the windows. He had left the light on so as not to draw attention to the rear of the house. He got to the back door, opened it just wide enough to slip through, and closed it after him.

Leaving the kitchen light on was the mistake that turned out to be his undoing. It gave Fergus a glimpse of him, a crouching shadow moving toward his car.

"There he is by his car!" Fergus shouted and dropped to the ground.

Brandon dove for the shelter of the cellar door. Seymour raised the gun and in that split second knew that he no longer cared what happened to him. He fired two shots. Brandon needed only one shot back. He had been winning prizes for marksmanship on police ranges for years.

The gun flew out of Seymour's hand. He cried out and stumbled forward. Then he fell.

He was unconscious when they reached him. He died while Fergus was looking for a flashlight in his car.

"He's gone," Brandon said when Fergus came back to him. "We can't do anything for him now." He was kneeling beside Seymour. He got slowly to his feet.

Fergus left him there and went into the house. He didn't go into the sitting room. He looked in from the doorway and then went back to Brandon.

"You shot a murderer," he said. "Horbal is dead, too. You'd better go in and look. Room's turned upside down, money scattered all over the floor . . ."

The lieutenant glanced at him. "No matter what a person was, it's a hell of a thing to take a human life. Well . . ." He turned away from Seymour's sprawled body. "I suppose I'd better have a look at the one inside. Money scattered around, you said?"

"It must run into the thousands. Hundred-dollar bills, fifties, twenties."

They walked toward the house. "I'll have to call the resident officer you mentioned," Brandon said. "What'd you say his name was?"

"Krajeski. Sergeant Krajeski." Fergus came to a halt. "Rick?"

"Yes?'

"We've got to keep Andrea out of this. She's gone through enough."

Brandon stared at him. "How can we? What other reason would we have for being mixed up in it at all? It's way outside my jurisdiction."

"Well, there must be some story we can tell to protect Andrea. I can't let her be dragged through the mud on this."

"But, Fergus, the law—"

"As far as I'm concerned, this is a case where the law is a mere abstraction weighed against the ruin of her life. Both these rogues are dead, Rick. There's no question of arrest or trial for either of them."

"No, there isn't. But how could I, a police officer sworn to uphold the law, go along with a

248

cover up in a case that includes murder and blackmail?"

Fergus faced him stubbornly. "You're a police officer off duty, outside your own territory. You're here only because I asked you to come."

"Why did you ask me to come, though, if it's not on account of Miss Langdon?" Brandon shook his head. "There are two dead men here and I killed one of them myself. I have to tell Krajeski the truth. He wouldn't swallow any lies I told him, anyway. Don't forget, you've already talked to him."

"Yes, but I told him I knew nothing about Boyd except that he was a shady character, and that I'd never even heard of Horbal until the other day when I followed Boyd to this house. Why can't I say my interest grew out of an anonymous telephone tip? After all, I'm a newspaperman. Not just a political writer, a newspaperman. I write under a by-line, which means a good many people are familiar with my name and that I do get anonymous telephone tips now and then."

"All right, I'll buy that. But what is this informer supposed to have told you?"

Fergus, thinking aloud, said slowly, "Well, in the first place, I must have got the call the day Boyd moved to the Wilton because I began checking with Condon on him that night . . ."

Fergus's pause was lengthy. Then he said, "Gambling, Rick. That will do it. No matter what address Boyd gave at the Wilton, he was a drifter from God knows where. Horbal's only been back a few months from Nevada. Why couldn't there have been a connection between them out there?"

"Las Vegas, for instance?" Brandon's attitude was more receptive than it had been a minute or two earlier.

"Yes, Las Vegas. My informer didn't pin it down, though. He just said that if I was interested in a gambling ring from out of state I should check on Boyd. Which I did. Then I followed him here, saw money change hands, and went to Krajeski for information." Fergus spoke more confidently now as he warmed to his invention. "This morning I had another telephone tip that there would be a pay-off today. I went to you about it. Maybe you were skeptical but there was a Ridgeway angle so you agreed to look into it. From there on the story goes as it really happened: Condon's call to tell me Boyd had checked out of the hotel, my call to you, our trip here, and the rest of it just as it took place. What harm is done to anyone if it's told that way? The main facts are true. All we're doing is leaving Andrea out of it."

"Why didn't I notify Krajeski on the way? This is his bailiwick."

"When we got to Oldfield his car wasn't in the yard—I noticed it wasn't there when we went by—and you didn't feel you should track him down and take him away from whatever he was doing when the whole thing might be a will-o'-the-wisp, anyway. Of course you intended to get in touch with him immediately if there was anything to it."

Brandon was silent, testing the story in his own mind.

Fergus continued, "I would say the only thing we have to explain is our presence here. It's not up to us to produce a blue print of why Boyd killed Horbal or what their previous association was. We assume that a quarrel over the money led to the killing, but that's only an assumption. Who's to say something that happened back in Nevada isn't a part of it?"

"If that was our story, Miss Langdon wouldn't get her money back."

"It doesn't matter."

"It matters that, as part of the investigation, Ridgeway banks will be checked for deposits and withdrawals in the amount of fifty thousand."

"Oh." Fergus turned this problem over in his mind. Then he asked, "Why should all of it be left around for Krajeski to find? Before we get him here couldn't I pick some of it up and give it back to her? I could pick up half of it—even more than that—and then they'd be checking on deposits and withdrawals in the neighborhood of twenty thousand."

"If the whole fifty thousand is here."

"It must be. If it's not in the house it's on

251

Boyd or in his car."

"We couldn't touch Boyd or his car. They stay just as they are." Brandon paused. Then he said, "Fergus, you told me this morning that if the truth came out it was nothing that would make Miss Langdon liable to arrest. You're sure of that? I couldn't even listen to your plan if there was the least question of—"

"There isn't, Rick. But if the truth came out it would ruin her life just the same. To no purpose, none at all, except to provide the public with a sensation. As I told you, it was something that happened when she was very young, something with various complications that Boyd and Horbal used to blackmail her. With both of them dead there's nothing to be gained by breaking it wide open all these years later. She's been through enough tragedy already. Rick, I beg of you—"

"What if this thing went sour? What if it wouldn't stick?"

"Then it would become my responsibility, not yours. As far as you're concerned, all you ever have to know is what I told you about Boyd being mixed up in a gambling ring. As a conscientious police officer it was something you were bound to follow up. Beyond that, I certainly wouldn't involve you in it."

"No," Brandon said, his voice suddenly warm, "I know you wouldn't, Fergus."

They went over the story again, filling in details here and there. But in the main it stayed as

Fergus had improvised it. The burden of proof as to what had happened here tonight did not, after all, rest on them. If Sergeant Krajeski brought up the red-haired little boy who had been boarded with the Horbals years ago, Fergus could only hope to dismiss him as a side issue, a coincidence.

Brandon was satisfied with the story at last. Justice in the abstract had lost out against the claims of old friendship and the ruin of Andrea's life.

Fergus felt humble in gratitude.

They went into the house and stood in the sitting-room doorway, looking at the shambles of the room and Walt Horbal's body on the floor.

Brandon shook his head. "When thieves fall out —"

"Yes." Fergus spoke absently, his thoughts on Andrea. With this pair dead, she had nothing more to fear. The burden of remembering he could help her to carry.

For the rest of their lives, he thought.

He began to pick up Andrea's money.

Brandon went looking for the telephone.

MYSTERIES TO KEEP YOU GUESSING
by John Dickson Carr

CASTLE SKULL   (1974, $3.50)
The hand may be quicker than the eye, but ghost stories
didn't hoodwink Henri Bencolin. A very real murderer was
afoot in Castle Skull—a murderer who must be found before he strikes again.

IT WALKS BY NIGHT   (1931, $3.50)
The police burst in and found the Duc's severed head staring at them from the center of the room. Both the doors
had been guarded, yet the murderer had gone in and out
without having been seen!

THE EIGHT OF SWORDS   (1881, $3.50)
The evidence showed that while waiting to kill Mr. Dep-
ping, the murderer had calmly eaten his victim's dinner.
But before famed crime-solver Dr. Gideon Fell could serve
up the killer to Scotland Yard, there would be another
course of murder.

THE MAN WHO COULD NOT SHUDDER (1703, $3.50)
Three guests at Martin Clarke's weekend party swore they
saw the pistol lifted from the wall, levelled, and shot. *Yet
no hand held it*. It couldn't have happened—but there was
a dead body on the floor to prove that it had.

J.J. MARRIC MYSTERIES

time passes quickly . . . As *DAY* blends with *NIGHT* and *WEEK* flies into *MONTH*, Gideon must fit together the pieces of death and destruction before time runs out!

GIDEON'S DAY   (2721, $3.95)
They mysterious death of a young police detective is only the beginning of a bizarre series of events which end in the fatal knifing of a seven-year-old girl. But for commander George gideon of New Scotland Yard, it is all in a day's work!

GIDEON'S MONTH   (2766, $3.95)
A smudged page on his calendar, Gideon's month is blackened by brazen and bizarre offenses ranging from mischief to murder. Gideon must put a halt to the sinister events which involve the corruption of children and a homicidal housekeeper, before the city drowns in blood!

GIDEON'S NIGHT   (2734, $3.50)
When an unusually virulent pair of psychopaths leaves behind a trail of pain, grief, and blood, Gideon once again is on the move. This time the terror all at once comes to a head and he must stop the deadly duel that is victimizing young women and children — in only one night!

GIDEON'S WEEK   (2722, $3.95)
When battered wife Ruby Benson set up her killer husband for capture by the cops, she never considered the possibility of his escape. Now Commander George Gideon of Scotland Yard must save Ruby from the vengeance of her sadistic spouse . . . or die trying!

Available wherever paperbacks are sold, or order direct from the Publisher. Send cover price plus 50¢ per copy for mailing and handling to Zebra Books, Dept. 2969, 475 Park Avenue South, New York, N.Y. 10016. Residents of New York, New Jersey and Pennsylvania must include sales tax. DO NOT SEND CASH.